MIND OVER MATTER

#3 THE CURSE OF THE IDOL'S EYE

MIND OVER MATTER

MATTER

#3 THE CURSE OF THE IDOL'S EYE

CHERYL ZACH

AN AVON CAMELOT BOOK

AVON BOOKS
A division of
The Hearst Corporation
1350 Avenue of the Americas
New York, New York 10019

Copyright © 1997 by Cheryl Zach
Published by arrangement with the author
Visit our website at **http://AvonBooks.com**
Library of Congress Catalog Card Number: 96-95090
ISBN: 0-380-78354-1
RL: 4.5

First Avon Camelot Printing: May 1997

CAMELOT TRADEMARK REG. U.S. PAT. OFF. AND IN OTHER COUNTRIES, MARCA REGISTRADA, HECHO EN U.S.A.

Printed in the U.S.A.

OPM   10   9   8   7   6   5   4   3   2   1

Dedicated with love to
my son Quinn and his wife Cindy,
my daughter Michelle and her fiancé Brad,
wishing them all good fortune
in life's great adventure.

Contents

1
Strange Vision

The man on the pavement had a painted face. It was white, with streaks of black, and he wore a stark black-and-white costume. He didn't speak, his face curiously masklike, but he moved gracefully as he bent his body, "sitting" on an invisible chair while he read an invisible newspaper.

Watching from a few feet away, twelve-year-old Quinn McMann admired the mime's muscle control. A second mime in the group came up behind his companion and pulled the "chair" out from under the first performer. The mime with the white-and-black face tumbled backward.

The crowd broke into laughter and scattered applause. Quinn clapped, and his friend and cousin Jamie Anderson giggled.

"Not bad," Jamie said.

Quinn nodded. But as he watched the mime stand up again, his smile faded.

The mime's painted face suddenly blurred, and the bland markings changed, altered, became fierce and savage and evil. Instead of the mime's face, Quinn saw a skull—a leering, malevolent skull with an unearthly intelligence glinting through the empty eyeholes where darkness should have been.

The skull-face turned and looked straight at Quinn. Quinn felt beads of sweat break out on his forehead. Everything else around him faded into a strange darkness. He was alone, unprotected, and he could feel waves of evil emanating from the skull-mask.

No voice came from the image, but nonetheless Quinn seemed to detect currents of thought. The patterns in his head swirled, crimson and black, and form emerged, jumbled thoughts that spoke to him in meanings too subtle for words. *Evil, it was evil, and it hungered.* . . .

"Quinn, Quinn, what's wrong?" Someone was shaking him. "You're not going to pass out, are you? Talk to me!"

Slowly, the darkness faded. Quinn stood on the pavement of Seaport Village again, smelled the salty tang of sea air, and heard the chatter of the shoppers and tourists who crowded the sidewalk. The mimes had moved off, seeking others to entertain. Only Jamie remained beside him, grasping his arm.

"Quinn, what is it?" she asked anxiously. "You're white as—as that mime's face paint."

Quinn shuddered. He didn't want to talk about the strange vision; sharing it would make it seem too real. "I don't know," he said slowly. His tongue felt thick. "I feel—my stomach doesn't feel so good."

Jamie looked at him, her expression concerned. "We shouldn't have eaten all that candy from the last shop. Mom will be back soon to meet us for lunch. Then this afternoon we're all going over to Balboa Park to visit the museums. Will you be okay?"

Quinn had lived in Los Angeles with Jamie and her mother Maggie Anderson, a noted television reporter, since shortly after the death of his own parents. Maggie often traveled to report the news, and this week they were in San Diego. While Maggie reported on a statewide economic conference and interviewed business leaders, Quinn and Jamie had been enjoying the sights of San Diego.

Quinn swallowed hard, pushing back the nausea that had threatened to overwhelm him. Should he tell Jamie about his strange vision? What did it mean?

When he first came to live with them, Jamie had

scoffed at his emerging psychic powers. With her genius IQ, Jamie wanted logical thinking, not wild guesses, as she called his moments of psychic awareness. But the adventures they had shared since had made a believer out of her.

Still, he wasn't ready to talk about what he'd seen, not yet. Quinn looked around at the small shops and the relaxed family groups and couples who wandered through the seaside complex. A seagull floated overhead, riding an air current, its bright eyes searching for scraps of food. It was all so normal that his fear subsided.

Until Quinn saw the man watching him—a dark-haired man of medium height, wearing a neat brown suit. He looked normal enough, but his gaze on Quinn was intent, and something about him—something was not right. Quinn swallowed hard. Why were his psychic powers so unpredictable? The vision of the strange mask had been so strong; why couldn't he pin down what he felt about the stranger?

He shut his eyes, trying to concentrate, but it didn't help. When he opened them again, the man was gone. He was probably just another tourist. You're getting jumpy, Quinn told himself.

"I'm okay," he said to Jamie. "Let's go. Maybe food is just what I need."

They found Maggie waiting in the restaurant where they'd agreed to meet for lunch. She was talking into her cellular phone, but she waved at them from her table by the window. Quinn and Jamie walked across to join her.

Maggie folded the phone and stuck it into her briefcase. "Having fun?"

Jamie nodded, so Quinn didn't have to answer. "How'd your interviews go?" she asked her mother.

"Not bad. We got some good shots of the opening session, and another of a vigorous debate over water policies."

Quinn's thoughts wandered as Jamie and Maggie talked. Where had that strange vision come from, and what did it mean? He was glad when the waiter brought them a menu. He examined the choices for lunch and tried not to think of anything else.

After a hearty seafood meal, they went back to Maggie's Jeep and she drove them all to Balboa Park at the edge of the business district.

Quinn and Jamie had spent yesterday at the world-famous San Diego Zoo. This afternoon Maggie had suggested some museum visits.

"We don't have time to visit them all in one afternoon," Maggie explained. She handed them each an admissions passport as Quinn and Jamie looked over a list of the park's museums. "What do you want to see the most? We can choose from space, sports, old cars, model trains, natural history, art . . ."

"Maybe the science center?" Jamie suggested.

Quinn glanced around from the Moorish-style exhibit halls to the tall California Tower with its bell. Something stirred inside him, and he said without thinking, "I want to see the Museum of Man first. I'll meet you at the science center later."

Without waiting for a response, he walked rapidly across the park. A toddler was chasing a ball, and two teenagers held hands, but Quinn ignored everyone else around him.

The Museum of Man was housed in more than one building, but Quinn knew which way to go, even though he'd never been here before. And when he went inside, Quinn barely glanced at the diagram of exhibits. Somehow, he knew which room he wanted. He hurried past several displays, giving them only a quick look. Not until he reached a presentation labeled BELIEFS OF THE ANCIENT AMERICANS, did he pause.

The first object was a jade death mask of a long-ago Maya chieftain. Next he saw a snarling, stylized gold jaguar. But it was the third image that made Quinn stop, frozen, as his heart pounded.

The small clay figure was squat and menacing, and on its face it wore a skull-mask. The label on the museum display said, MICTLANTECUHTLI, AZTEC LORD OF THE UNDERWORLD.

The vision that had overwhelmed him while he watched the mime flashed through his mind again, and Quinn shuddered. Why had an image similar to this skull-faced artifact called out to him? What was going on?

2
Skull-Mask

"Quinn, what's wrong? Are you sick again?"

It was Jamie, and Maggie was there, too. They had followed him into this museum instead of going on to the science center.

Quinn shook his head. How could he explain that a small artifact in a museum display had reawakened the formless terror that had overwhelmed him this morning? He pointed toward the display.

Maggie looked into the case, then back at him. She felt his forehead. "This is interesting, but you're pale, and you feel clammy. If you're not feeling well, the museums can wait. We'd better take you back to the hotel."

Quinn didn't argue. They drove back to the hotel in silence. When they reached their own suite of rooms, Maggie said, "Why don't you lie down for a while? If you're not better later, I'll call a doctor."

"I'm okay," Quinn muttered. But he went into the second bedroom and stretched out across his bed. Quinn shut his eyes and tried not to think, not to remember.

When Maggie came to check on him an hour later, she touched his cheek gently. "Good, you don't feel feverish."

"I'm okay now," Quinn said. The strange fear had subsided again. He felt silly; he'd never had psychic visions quite like this, and he'd wished they would stop.

"Rest awhile, just to be sure," Maggie told him. "It's probably just an upset stomach."

Her phone buzzed, and Maggie went through the connecting door. They were staying in a small suite with a living room in the middle and a bedroom and bath on each side. Maggie and Jamie shared the other bedroom, and Quinn had a room to himself. The door was half open, and Quinn could hear parts of the conversation.

"I wasn't going to work this afternoon, Carol," Maggie said. "I—oh, all right. I'll see what I can do."

Quinn grinned. It didn't take a psychic's ability to know that Maggie's job was unpredictable, and news stories could happen at any time.

When she looked back into the room, Quinn gave her a thumbs-up. "I'm okay. You don't have to hang around," he told her.

"I'll check on you occasionally," Maggie told him. "Jamie, call my cellular phone if you need me."

When he heard the door shut behind her, Quinn sat up. Who wanted to lie around all day? He found Jamie in the next room, curled up on the couch with a book.

"Want to go for a swim?" he asked.

"Sure, you up to it?" She closed her book and looked him up and down.

"I'm okay. Let me get my swimsuit." Quinn shut the door and dug through his bag until he found his suit, then changed quickly.

When Jamie knocked on the door, he was ready. Jamie had her own swimsuit on, and she had tied her shoulder-length red hair into a ponytail. She had already grabbed a couple of towels and a small plastic ball.

"I left a message for Mom, telling her where we'll be," she told him.

They took the elevator down to the lobby floor and walked out the side doors to the big swimming pool. A mother and two little kids played at the shallow end, and a balding man sat on a lounge chair and read a newspaper.

Jamie dropped the towels on an empty chaise

lounge. She walked to the diving board, tossed him the ball, and dove expertly into the pool.

Quinn sat on the edge of the pool, waiting for her to surface. When she came up, Jamie rubbed the water out of her eyes.

"Here." He tossed her the ball, then slipped into the water. Its chlorine-scented warmth enveloped him, and the sensations drove any thought of the fearful vision out of his head.

Before he was ready, Jamie threw the lightweight plastic ball back; it bounced off his forehead.

"My point," Jamie called.

The ball floated, swaying on the surface of the water. Quinn grabbed it and swam closer, ready to take his revenge.

Laughing, Jamie retreated.

Quinn thought briefly how nice it was to have a friend, a quasi cousin, a partner. He'd spent so many years as a loner, never quite accepted by the other kids because he seemed so different. Jamie, with her super brain and extensive vocabulary, had suffered her share of teasing from her peers, too. Now his life was so different. Despite his lingering sadness over the loss of his parents, Quinn was happy.

He tossed the ball. Jamie reached for it and missed; it bopped her on the chin.

"My point." Quinn laughed and dove under the water before Jamie could throw the ball back.

They played a vigorous game of water ball, with their own special rules, until the white hotel phone at the side of the pool beeped.

Jamie pulled herself out of the pool, grabbed a towel and rubbed her face and hands, then walked across to answer. She spoke briefly into the phone, then waved at Quinn.

"Mom will be back soon, and she wants to talk to us. It sounds imperative; we'd better get dressed."

Quinn was used to Jamie's big words. Grinning, he swam to the edge of the pool and climbed the metal ladder. He took the other towel and hastily rubbed himself down. Then they walked across the lobby and took the elevator up to their rooms.

Upstairs, he took a quick shower to get rid of the chlorine smell, then dressed in a navy knit shirt and khaki slacks instead of his jeans. Maggie usually took them to a sit-down restaurant for dinner.

He heard Maggie come in as he combed his still-damp hair, and he hurried to the living room.

"Feeling better? Good," she said when he nodded. "We'll go out to dinner in a while. My producer told me about this great restaurant downtown. But first, someone is coming over to see you."

"Me?" Startled, Quinn wasn't sure he had heard her right. Maggie knew lots of important, sometimes even famous people, but who would want to meet Quinn?

Before he could ask, Jamie joined them, dressed but with her red hair still wrapped in a towel. She asked the question that was in Quinn's mind, too. "Who wants to meet Quinn?" she demanded. "And why?"

Her mother smiled. "Nathan Verdun. He's an archaeologist who sometimes teaches classes at the university here. He's highly regarded in the scholastic community."

"Archaeologist?" Jamie's eyes widened. "You mean like that guy in the adventure movies with the leather jacket and the whip? Wow."

Maggie laughed. "Not exactly, I doubt Nathan Verdun has people chasing him through jungles and deserts. And I don't know why he wants to talk to Quinn, but I'm sure he has a good reason."

Quinn swallowed, wondering what this could mean. "When is he coming?"

Maggie looked at her watch. "Any minute."

Jamie touched the towel on her head. "Yikes, be right back." She ran toward the other bathroom, and in a moment, Quinn heard the whirl of the blow-dryer.

Why did this Nathan guy want to talk to him? Quinn wrinkled his nose, thinking. Archaeologists dealt with old civilizations, right?

With a sinking feeling, Quinn wondered if Nathan Verdun studied the ancient Americans, like the Aztecs, for instance.

Quinn didn't know much about the Aztec culture. Remembering the museum exhibit, he wasn't sure he wanted to.

A knock sounded at the hall door.

3
A Plea for Help

By the time Jamie had dried her damp hair, put a dollop of gel on her palm, and pushed the red waves into some kind of order, she could hear a man's voice in the living room. She couldn't miss this. She hurried back to the main room.

Her mom was smiling at a tall man with blond hair and gray eyes. To Jamie's disappointment he was wearing an ordinary business suit, not a leather jacket, and he didn't look a bit like a movie star.

"I've heard a lot about you," Maggie was saying. "Some of my friends at the university know you—Joanna in the history department, and Tom Rollins at the library."

The two were shaking hands, and it seemed to Jamie that the archaeologist held her mother's hand for a second too long. And from the look of it, Maggie didn't mind. Jamie frowned. She knew that her mom was beautiful, but she didn't have time for an admirer. Between her demanding job and her family, Maggie's life was full enough, wasn't it? Anyhow, her mom was too old for silly romantic stuff. She wished she could tell Nathan Verdun that. Instead, Jamie smiled hastily when Maggie turned toward her.

"This is my daughter Jamie."

Nathan held out his hand, and Jamie reached for it, then almost too late remembered her gel-sticky palm. She waved at him instead and tried to make her smile genuine. Nathan turned to Quinn.

"And this is our cousin Quinn McMann, who's part of our family, now," Maggie said.

Quinn and Nathan shook hands briefly. Quinn's expression was noncommittal, but Jamie thought his shoulders looked tense. What was he thinking? What was this all about, anyhow?

Maggie waved their visitor toward the sitting area, and everyone sat down. Jamie perched on the arm of her mom's chair and watched the stranger, who looked as if he were collecting his thoughts.

"I suppose I should tell you first that I've heard a little about the incident that occurred at the Malone Museum in Los Angeles, how you were able to stop the theft of priceless art treasures, including the mummy of the young prince."

What had the scientist heard? Jamie looked quickly at Quinn, but his expression was still guarded. Very little of the real story had come out in the press. Quinn had said that no one would believe what had really happened, anyhow—how Quinn had been haunted by a mummy. The police detectives certainly didn't.

"I have friends in museum circles," Nathan explained. "So I've been told some of the, umm, extra details. For example, I know that this young man"—he glanced at Quinn—"has some interesting powers."

Quinn raised his chin. "Not everyone believes in psychic abilities," he said evenly. "Not even in ESP."

"I know," Nathan agreed, "and not everyone who claims to be a psychic is genuine. But I do believe in this kind of mental power, even if we don't understand it completely. And I need your help."

He spoke quietly, but the words seemed charged with their own urgency. Quinn sat up straighter, and Jamie took a deep breath.

"Tell me what this is all about," Quinn said.

"It started with a stabbing down at the docks," Nathan told them.

Maggie frowned, looking from Nathan to Quinn. "Surely that's a matter for the police?"

Nathan nodded. "They're investigating, but the stabbing led authorities to a shipment of ancient artifacts, mostly Aztec and Toltec, smuggled out of Mexico and on their way to Japan, to be sold to the highest bidder, I imagine. When the police discovered the hidden cargo, they called me in to identify and value the objects."

"Are they valuable?" Jamie interrupted, remembering the gold and jewels they had seen so briefly in the Balboa Park Museum. Wow, maybe this *would* be a little like a movie adventure, after all.

"Priceless," Nathan told them. "Aside from their historic importance, the Aztecs used gold and precious gems in their sculptures. This cache, probably just discovered, is a real prize, and if a fight hadn't broken out among the ship's crew, authorities here would never have found it before it was gone forever. Now most of the shipment has been confiscated, ready to be returned to Mexican authorities. But one piece disappeared before the police could impound it."

Quinn said, very quietly, "This missing object—does it look like a human skull? Maybe a mask shaped like a skull?"

Everyone looked at him. Jamie exclaimed in

surprise, "Like the little clay figure we saw at the museum?"

Instead of answering her, Quinn glanced at the archaeologist and waited for his answer.

Nathan had raised his eyebrows, and he regarded Quinn with evident respect. "It's a skull-mask, yes, probably of the Aztec god of death. But it's not made of clay. According to the crew's account, this piece is hammered gold, and worth a huge sum."

"We saw a similar clay mask on an Aztec figure in a museum this afternoon," Jamie explained, glancing at Quinn.

But he shook his head. "I first saw a vision of it this morning, while we were at Seaport Village."

"What? Why didn't you tell me?" Jamie demanded indignantly before she thought.

Maggie gave her a stern look, and Jamie bit back the rest of what she wanted to say. But she and Quinn were supposed to be partners, using their individual mental powers as a team. She'd even thought of a name for their specialized strengths—Mind Over Matter. Why had Quinn not shared his weird experience with her? She folded her arms, trying not to look as hurt as she felt.

Nathan said, "I was hoping you could help me find the mask and return it to the authorities. The police don't deal with the theft of antiquities every day. I'm afraid if we don't do something, it will never be recovered."

Quinn looked somber. "It's too dangerous to ignore," he said. "I"—he glanced at Jamie—"we will help you."

And Jamie felt better, at least, until she saw the warning in Quinn's blue eyes.

Did he say "dangerous"?

4
Echoes of Fear

"I want to help," Quinn repeated. "We both do." He looked across at Jamie, who nodded emphatically. Quinn knew his partner in detection—no way that Jamie would miss a good adventure.

Maggie didn't look as certain. "I don't know about this," she said slowly. "I understand the importance of the case, but I don't like the idea of the kids being involved with violent criminals."

Jamie looked indignantly at her mother, who met her daughter's gaze squarely. After a moment, Jamie looked down, but her lips drooped.

"I wouldn't think of taking them into contact with the suspected thief," Nathan assured Maggie. "Actually, the man who stabbed his fellow crew member isn't a hardened criminal. At least, he has no record of violence before this incident."

"See," Jamie muttered.

"I just want to take Quinn—and Jamie—to the place where the mask was stolen, and see if Quinn can get any impressions that might help us find its current hiding place, or give us an idea of who has it now."

Maggie considered and finally nodded slowly. "All right, I suppose that can't hurt."

Jamie sighed in relief, and Quinn felt both anticipation and a prickling of fear. An unpleasant memory of this morning's strange vision flashed through his mind. He couldn't forget the waves of evil that he had felt emanating from the golden skull-mask. This was no ordinary icon. Somehow, it held more than long-buried memories.

He blinked. Nathan was waiting for him to answer, and Quinn hadn't heard the question.

"When would you be ready to go?" Nathan repeated.

"Right now is fine with me," Quinn told him, and Jamie nodded her agreement.

"Good, I like a man of action." The archaeologist smiled, and Quinn decided that this guy was all right.

He told Jamie so as they headed for the elevator, one step behind Nathan and Maggie. Maggie had decided to come with them; she still didn't seem to completely trust their safety in this new investigation.

To his surprise, Jamie shrugged. "Maybe," she murmured, glancing toward the tall scientist. "I'm not so sure."

They couldn't discuss him with Nathan so close. In the elevator, Quinn wondered about Jamie's unusual antipathy. Why didn't she like the man?

Then he looked at Nathan, whose eyes met Maggie's often as they talked. Maggie smiled, and Quinn saw Jamie stiffen as she watched the two adults. Uh-huh, Quinn thought. So that's it.

They all rode together in Nathan's Land Rover. He turned back toward the ocean. As they neared the water, they saw rows of tuna boats and pleasure craft tied up along the docks, dwarfed by an occasional cruise ship that loomed over the smaller vessels. Farther along the harbor front, rows of gray navy ships were topped with forbidding weaponry. Quinn began to feel uneasy.

He was with friends, with Jamie and Maggie and Nathan, Quinn told himself firmly. And the mask was just an old piece of gold. He refused to be frightened by these weird visions.

Nathan turned the vehicle into an alley behind a row of shabby warehouses and parked halfway down. He motioned to the warehouse in front of them.

"The police traced the mask here after it left the cargo ship. They believe the man who stole it hid it inside, but he came back and retrieved it, maybe late yesterday. Where it's been taken now, we don't know."

They got out and approached the warehouse, where a bored-looking guard was just locking the side door.

"Hi, Nate," the man said. "You back again? What'd you do—bring a field trip, this time?" He glanced indulgently toward Quinn and the others.

Quinn stood up straighter. Field trip, huh? He'd love to solve this case right under the noses of the police; that would show all the adults not to count him out just because he was only twelve.

Nathan said, "No, not exactly. But we'd like to look around inside, if you don't mind."

The security guard unlocked the door again and waved them in. "Go ahead. The cops have already taken fingerprints and all that. There's nothing much left to see."

Nathan led them inside. The warehouse was a big, roughly finished building with metal walls and a tall ceiling. A few boxes and crates were stacked at one side; otherwise, it was empty.

The archaeologist led them to the corner where a wooden crate sat, its lid pried hastily off and left lying at an angle on the floor.

"This is where we believe the mask was hidden briefly. When Carlos, the man who was stabbed, identified the man who attacked him as Antoine, police investigators discovered that Antoine had a cousin who worked as a security guard at this warehouse. When they brought the cousin in for questioning, he admitted giving Antoine a key. But by the time the police got to the warehouse, he'd moved the icon again."

Quinn braced himself, then walked closer and touched the wooden crate. He shut his eyes and opened his mind, and he felt something at once.

Like an echo of a loud noise, the impression of the mask had not yet faded. It had lain here, wrapped in grubby newspaper, but its brutal golden splendor, its empty eyeholes, were still visible to Quinn as he looked with that inner sense that he could never quite explain. And even more than its physical presence, the still tangible impression of malevolence also lingered. Quinn shivered and stepped back, breaking his connection.

"Quinn, are you all right?" Maggie asked, concern in her voice.

He took a deep breath and nodded. What good could he be to investigators if he couldn't control this nausea? His stomach rolled, and he knew it was because he'd glimpsed something evil. If he wanted to help people like his dad had done, he had to be stronger. Quinn forced himself to step closer and touch the box again.

It was hard to see beyond the mask itself. Its

power, even this faint psychic echo, was overwhelming. But Quinn reached further and got a faint impression of the man who had stolen the golden idol.

"He's afraid," Quinn said, very low, barely aware that he was speaking his thoughts aloud. "But he's also greedy; he doesn't want to give up this treasure. He knows the police are after him, and he's worried about getting away. He's stolen a truck from the docks, no, I think it's a small van, and he left here—only this morning, not yesterday."

His voice faded, and Quinn felt the mask's force once again overwhelm the pale impression he had of the thief. It was hungry . . . hungry. . . .

Quinn stepped back, unable to bear the feelings that the mask had left behind. It was too sinister; he didn't want to know the rest.

He looked up at Nathan. Had he disappointed the archaeologist? But Quinn saw the tall man smile.

"Great job, Quinn. Now we know a little more to help the police track down the thief. Maybe with luck, we'll soon have the mask back."

Quinn nodded, but he suppressed a shiver. He turned to Jamie for reassurance—the adults had moved a few steps toward the door—but to his surprise Jamie frowned at him.

"Is that all you could come up with?"

Quinn blinked, then flushed. "Hey, I'm not a computer, you know. What did you expect? Print in the question and the answer flashes on my forehead?"

He heard the sarcasm in his own voice and wasn't surprised when she stomped off. Jamie followed her mom and the archaeologist out of the building.

She didn't usually act like that. What was wrong with Jamie? Quinn walked outside, trying not to show how weak his knees felt. If Maggie knew how much he dreaded any contact with the skull-mask, she might not let him continue.

Outside, Quinn was glad to take a deep breath, even though the air smelled faintly fishy from the nearby docks. It seemed to clear his mind, and he thought of something else.

"Dr. Verdun?"

"You can call me Nate," the archaeologist told him. "What is it?"

"I just thought—this morning, when I had the vision of the skull-mask, we were at Seaport Village. If Antoine moved the mask then, he might have driven past that area. If so, it would give you some idea of which direction he was headed."

"Good thinking, Quinn," Nate said. "I'm going to call the detective in charge of this case and have him check for stolen vehicles. If we pin

27

down the van that Antoine is using, that will give the police something specific to watch for."

Nate turned back to speak to Maggie, and Quinn walked toward the main street, ready to leave the warehouse with its tainted atmosphere behind. Jamie hurried to catch up with him.

"Quinn, I'm sorry. I didn't mean what I said. I don't even know—"

She was interrupted by a sudden shrill scream. "Help!"

5
Attack

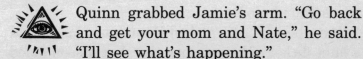 Quinn grabbed Jamie's arm. "Go back and get your mom and Nate," he said. "I'll see what's happening."

He ran toward the street. With no great surprise, he heard Jamie's footsteps just behind him. Didn't she ever listen? Getting help was the sensible thing to do, but logical as Jamie could be, her curiosity was even stronger.

On the street, Quinn saw an olive-skinned girl about their own age, with thick dark hair and brown eyes wide with fear. Three teens in slouchy jeans and ripped T-shirts circled her like hungry coyotes.

"Leave me alone!" the girl shrieked; her voice vibrant with fear.

"What's the matter, can't take the heat?" the tallest teen jeered. He reached for the girl and

29

yanked a strand of her curly brown hair. She winced.

Quinn stepped forward. "Back off," he said, trying to keep his voice calm. They were all bigger and heavier than he, and there were three of them. But he couldn't walk away and leave this girl to be tormented, maybe attacked. Where was that security guard when he was needed?

The first teen twisted to stare at Quinn, who stood just behind him. "Oh, gee," he said with heavy sarcasm. "Look at the white knight charging to the rescue. You impressed, guys? Maria, who's your hero?"

The whole group watched Quinn now. Maria had a faint flicker of hope in her eyes, but it soon faded as the other boys stepped closer to Quinn.

"What does it matter to you what we do, Anglo?" the first teen asked, his tone menacing.

Quinn felt his hands curl into fists. He took a deep breath, watching the trio line up in front of him. He knew a little karate, but against streetwise punks like this, he doubted that his limited skills would buy him much time. *Run away*, a voice inside him seemed to whisper. *What business is it of yours?*

But he couldn't leave, not when he saw Maria's face pale with fear.

"My mom is calling the police on her cellular phone," Jamie said clearly. She stepped out of the alley's shadows; Quinn could see her from the corner of his eye. "They'll be here any minute."

The three teens glanced at each other, then down the street. "We'll be back," the first teen said.

They ambled away, with one eye on the end of the street, not quite running. When they turned into another alleyway and disappeared, Quinn took a deep breath.

Maria wiped away the tears of fear that still glittered on her cheeks. *"Gracias,"* she said. "I only came down to bring my father his lunch. He works two streets over in another warehouse. I was on my way home. I hadn't run into those honchos before."

Jamie stepped closer and patted Maria's arm. "That was scary," she agreed. "Come on, my mom will give you a lift home. Those guys might come back."

Especially since Jamie's call to the police was only a threat—she'd never gone back to inform Maggie, Quinn thought. Trust Jamie to come through with a good bluff.

"Let's go," he agreed. Jamie and Maria hurried back toward the Land Rover and the waiting adults. Quinn was about to follow when he saw the man in the shadows.

It was the man in the brown suit again. Quinn tensed. Who was he, and what was he doing here?

The man stepped forward; he had been hidden by the edge of the warehouse. "I was coming to help you with those punks, but your friend scared them off."

Quinn's eyes narrowed. "Who are you?"

The man reached inside his jacket, and Quinn braced himself, expecting a weapon. Instead, the stranger pulled out a leather wallet. He flipped it open to reveal an ID. The words were in Spanish. Quinn tried to decipher it, then gave up.

"Mexican police, on special assignment," the man explained. "I am Lieutenant Pajaro." He slipped the wallet back into his pocket, and Quinn relaxed.

"Are you working with the San Diego police and Nate Verdun?" he asked.

The lieutenant frowned. "All the police do not know. It is necessary that only a few know that I am here. I am—what do you say—beneath the blanket."

Under cover. Quinn nodded. If the Mexican authorities were trying to find the stolen art, that made sense. "But Nate is helping—"

"I do not trust this scientist. He may not be all that he says he is," Lieutenant Pajaro said, his tone very low. "It is better if he does not know my identity until I am sure about him."

Surprised, Quinn blinked, not sure what to answer. He heard Maggie call him and he looked over his shoulder.

"Coming."

When he turned back to say good-bye, the Mexican officer had already slipped away. This guy took his undercover status seriously, Quinn thought. He went back to rejoin the others.

Maggie looked anxious. "Are you all right? Jamie told us about those boys."

"I'm fine." Should he mention the policeman? Maybe not, Quinn thought, glancing at Nate Verdun. But the archaeologist had seemed so frank. Surely, he wasn't hiding anything. If he worked with the police—but then, they hadn't actually seen him with the San Diego police, had they? They only had his word for his involvement.

Later, after they had dropped Maria safely at her home, Nate drove them back to their hotel and said good-bye.

"You've been a big help," the archaeologist said. "I'll keep you up to date on the case. Quinn, if you think of anything else that might help, give me a call."

The archaeologist took a business card from his pocket and handed it to Quinn. Quinn put the card carefully into his own pocket. Why not just call the police, he thought, dark suspicions of the scientist newly planted in his mind.

"I need to go down to the television studio,"

Maggie told the two when they were back in their suite. "You guys stay here, okay? No roaming around town."

"Sure, Mom," Jamie agreed. After Maggie had left, Quinn turned to Jamie.

"I need to tell you something," he said. He didn't care what Lieutenant Pajaro had said; Jamie was his partner. Besides, if he kept her in the dark again, she'd really be ticked off.

He explained about the stranger, his unexpected reappearance, and what he had said.

"Ha, I knew this Nate guy wasn't as perfect as he appeared," Jamie said.

"Why? Just because he's making eyes at Maggie?"

Jamie frowned at him. "Of course not. My mom wouldn't like anyone that obvious."

Quinn wasn't so sure, but they were getting off the track. "Nate may be exactly what he says he is. Pajaro said he wasn't sure; I guess he's still checking. But in the meantime, what about the mask? If it turns up, who do we tell?"

"Do you think you can find it?" Jamie asked eagerly.

"I don't know, but I have this strong feeling about it—it seems to call to me," Quinn said, swallowing hard at the memory. There, he had said it.

Jamie's eyes widened. "What does it say?"

"Not in words, exactly, just feelings—it's hungry, Jamie. And it's evil, I'm sure of it."

Jamie folded her arms. "Then we really have to locate it."

Quinn was about to nod, but a yawn surprised him, instead.

"You look beat," Jamie told him. "What's it like, Quinn, when you do that—that psychic thing?"

Quinn shut his eyes for an instant. "I can't really explain. It's kind of like seeing from the inside. But it takes a lot out of me. I feel exhausted, afterwards, drained."

"Is this the way your dad did it?"

Quinn nodded, feeling a surge of pride. "That was the best sighting I've ever done," he told her, adding honestly, "though I think it's partly because the skull-mask itself is so strong."

"How do you mean strong? It's just an object," Jamie argued. "A piece of gold, Aztec artwork."

Quinn was too tired to try to make her understand. "There's something connected to it, strong feelings, something."

Jamie looked thoughtful. "Go ahead and crash. I'm going to look up the Aztecs and see what I can find out. Mom left her laptop here, and I can hook up the modem on the hotel phone."

Jamie opened the laptop computer and was soon absorbed in the flickering screen.

Eyelids drooping, Quinn went to his own bedroom and lay down across the bed. He shut his eyes and tried to relax. But he couldn't leave the mask behind, even in sleep. He knew it was a dream, not real, but when the golden skull-mask appeared, he drew back in horror. It was too vivid, and the empty eyeholes seemed to look at him. . . .

Cold with fear, Quinn tried to push away the apparition. "You're evil, and we're going to find you," he told it silently. "I'm getting closer all the time."

And the mask's metal mouth curved upward into a grotesque smile.

6
Rivers of Blood

Quinn struggled to wake. It was a dream, it was only a dream, he told himself. It can't hurt me.

But the mask's golden face was too close. The strange twisted smile leered at him, and always, the empty eyeholes watched. It loomed closer and closer. . . .

Quinn woke at last, gasping. It had been too real, too menacing, that image of the mask. Was it really aware of him? Did it know that Quinn was searching for the stolen artifact? Or was it only a dream, his own fears taking shape inside his mind?

Jamie knocked on his bedroom door.

"Come in," Quinn said, pushing himself up. Glad to be distracted from his nightmare, he swung himself off the bed. But when he saw Jamie's face, he paused.

"What's wrong?"

"I've been looking up the Aztecs, Quinn." Jamie swallowed hard. "They built splendid cities larger than old London, they crafted detailed artwork, and they loved flowers. But their religion was based on human sacrifice. Oh, Quinn, they would cut the beating hearts out of their victims—the altars ran red with rivers of blood."

Quinn shut his eyes for a moment; he could see the leering mask all too clearly. It was this kind of evil he had sensed in the artifact. Opening his eyes, Quinn glanced at Jamie; she looked pale. "Tell you what, let's go back to the pool and try to forget all this for a while."

Jamie nodded. "Deal."

Yet later, even in the pool, Quinn couldn't completely push away that sense of evil lurking. It was out there, somewhere, and he had to find it.

After a quiet dinner and a movie with Maggie and Jamie, Quinn found it hard to sleep. He was up early the next morning, waiting for a reasonable time to call Nate. How could he check out Nate's status with the police and make sure he was what he said he was? Quinn could just call the police department, but he'd likely get the same reaction from them that he had from the warehouse guard. Would they even talk to him about a sensitive case? Maggie might be able to find out, but Quinn wanted to do this himself.

He couldn't forget the warehouse guard's grin. Quinn had something to prove.

Pushing the buttons on the phone, he caught the archaeologist in his office. "Hi, this is Quinn."

"Quinn, have you thought of something new?" Nate sounded hopeful.

"No, sorry," Quinn said. "But I'd like to talk to the man who was stabbed, the crewman on the ship where the mask was hidden."

There was silence for a moment as Nate considered. "All right, I'll set it up with the police. I have classes at the university all morning, but I can take you this afternoon . . ."

"We can go on our own. There's nothing dangerous about this guy, is there?"

"No, shouldn't be." The archaeologist gave Quinn information about the hospital, and Quinn made notes on the hotel's memo pad, then ripped off the sheet and stuck it into his pocket.

"The police are on the lookout for a stolen van," Nate told him. "They checked the list of stolen vehicles, and sure enough, a brown van was stolen from the docks. We owe that clue to you. Maybe we'll have the mask back soon."

"Maybe," Quinn murmured, remembering the leering vision of his dream. He hung up the phone. "And maybe not." But he felt better. Surely Nate couldn't have done all this without a genuine connection with the police. Pajaro was being too careful, that's all, Quinn told himself.

When he went into the suite's living room, he found Maggie with a cup of coffee in her hand, glancing through her briefcase.

"I have two interviews today. I'll check back with you guys at lunchtime," she told him. "Stay close to the hotel."

Quinn nodded. Close was a relative term, he told himself as Maggie swept out the door. His dad had always trusted Quinn and had never tried to keep tabs on him every minute, and Maggie didn't, either. Sometimes, though, there were things you had to do.

He walked across the room and pounded on the other bedroom door. "Get up, or you'll be left behind," he called to Jamie. "I'm going to check out a hunch."

That brought her out within minutes, hastily dressed in T-shirt and jeans, her red hair still tousled. Quinn grinned at her sleepy expression.

"Where are we going?" Jamie demanded, rubbing her eyes.

A couple of muffins remained on the tray that Maggie had ordered from room service. Quinn handed Jamie a muffin, picked up the other one for himself, and they headed for the door. "I'll tell you when we find the bus stop."

They were both accustomed to finding their

way around Los Angeles, so the busy streets of San Diego didn't scare them. Quinn stopped in the lobby to double-check his directions to the hospital with the hotel staff, and the concierge provided a small map of San Diego.

On the bus, Jamie gulped down the rest of her muffin, then wiped her fingers on her jeans. "You think this guy in the hospital can tell us something?"

"It's worth checking out. And it gives Nate the chance to prove he's working with the police."

Jamie frowned. "Maybe he's fooled the police. Was this just an excuse to test Nathan? You know the police have already interrogated Manuel."

Quinn shrugged. "I know, but I want to talk to him myself. Trust me, okay?"

Jamie nodded and stared out the window at the passing street. When they reached the hospital, a tall building of white concrete and sunlit glass, Quinn headed for the elevator.

"Nate told me the floor where Manuel Ortema is being held," he explained to Jamie.

The archaeologist had also alerted the hospital. Quinn and Jamie were on the list of people allowed to speak to Manuel, who was still under police custody. Still, the nurse lifted her brows when Quinn walked up to the nurse's station. "I was expecting you to be older," she said, adjusting her glasses.

"I'm aging every minute," Quinn murmured.

Jamie giggled, and the nurse pursed her lips. But she allowed them to continue, as did the policeman at the door.

Inside the hospital room, a man with graying dark hair and a faded blue hospital gown lay in the bed. A television droned up above the bed, but the man didn't seem to be listening.

"Señor Ortema?" Quinn asked politely. "Could we speak to you, *por favor*?"

"You are from the police?" The merchant sailor lifted his head and stared at them suspiciously.

"Not exactly, but we're helping them with the case," Quinn tried to explain. "Maybe you could tell me about the attack?"

Manual shook his head. "No, Antoine is my friend. Once he pulled me from the ocean when a big wave knocked me off the deck—there were sharks. I will not send him to jail."

"But he tried to kill you," Jamie burst in impatiently. "How can you protect him?"

Quinn could see the white bandages beneath the loose-fitting blue gown. He waited for the man to answer. The sailor took his time, then spoke slowly, not quite meeting their eyes.

"Who is to say? We all have moments of madness. But he saved my life once, and we worked together for twelve years. I know he didn't mean to kill me."

"Then tell me about the mask," Quinn suggested.

This time, Manuel's fear was obvious. Shuddering, the old sailor crossed himself. "That—that is evil. It reaches out and calls to you. No, I do not speak of such things. Leave it to the police, and the priests, perhaps. I only want to forget."

"Can you?" Quinn asked softly. "Can you sleep at night, without seeing that golden face?"

Manuel's face twisted into a grimace, and above his head the monitor's jagged lines suddenly spiked. A nurse appeared in the doorway and hurried to the bed. She reached to check Manuel's pulse, then frowned at them as they stood beside the bed.

"He's had enough excitement for today. It's time for you to leave."

They walked out silently, and as they rode the elevator down to the main floor, Jamie threw up her hands. "We wasted our time. That wasn't very illuminating," she said, her tone disgusted.

"Speak in two syllables, please," Quinn told her, grinning. "I think it was."

"Why? He didn't say anything."

"He said Antoine was his friend."

"Some friend—he tried to kill him, just for an old piece of gold," Jamie pointed out.

"A very valuable piece of gold," Quinn reminded her.

"But I think it's more than that. Look at how scared Manuel is. And as for the mask's power, why did you snap at me yesterday inside the warehouse?"

Jamie flushed. She leaned over to tie her shoelace and didn't meet his gaze. "I—I just—I don't know. What's that got to do with anything? Are you saying this mask can control the people around it? Like a curse or something?"

The elevator doors slid open, and they walked out into the lobby. Visitors and patients sat on rows of chairs in front of a television set.

Before Quinn had decided how to answer, how much of his half-formed suspicions to share, a news bulletin flashed across the screen. Quinn stopped to listen.

"A freak accident has tied up traffic at the edge of the business district," the reporter said. "Our traffic helicopter spotted a lethal accident in the making."

As Quinn watched, the film showed a large truck veer off course for no apparent reason, crushing the front of a smaller truck and two cars before it rolled to a stop.

"Ambulances are rushing to the scene, and the reason for the accident is still under investigation," the reporter said.

Quinn paid close attention as they rolled the bit of tape again, but this time he watched the corner of the screen.

"Look!" He grabbed Jamie's arm in his excitement. "Just before the trucker goes berserk, see—on the street a few cars back—it's a brown van!"

7
Whom to Trust?

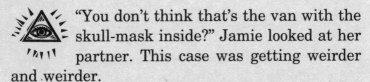 "You don't think that's the van with the skull-mask inside?" Jamie looked at her partner. This case was getting weirder and weirder.

Quinn nodded. "I've got to call Nate," he said.

"But what if he's in this for his own reasons?" Jamie argued. "I know you think he's okay, but maybe he wants the gold mask for himself. Remember what Lieutenant Pajaro said."

"Then what do we do?"

"We'll call the police," Jamie said.

They found public phones at the edge of the hospital lobby and Quinn dialed 911.

"It's about the big accident on Market Street . . . Oh, it's already been reported. Yes, I know, but—no, I'm not hurt, it's just . . ."

Quinn sighed and hung up the phone. "They

want the lines clear; they won't listen. I think we have to call Nate, Jamie, even if we're not sure."

This time, Quinn dialed the number on the archaeologist's business card. But Nate was still in class. Quinn left a message, then hung up the phone, looking frustrated.

"We can't just wait here," Jamie said. "Come on, let's see if we can get any closer."

They walked outside the hospital to the nearest bus stop. For once, they caught a bus right away. When the traffic slowed, backed up by the accident, Quinn motioned to Jamie. "Let's get off here."

They stepped off the bus at the next stop and walked closer. Two ambulances and three police cars added to the confusion as cars honked and impatient drivers sat frowning inside their cars.

The police had blocked off a section of the street, but even from where they stood, Jamie could see the wreck. A paramedic hurried forward, pushing a stretcher. Quinn folded his arms.

Jamie looked at the crumpled metal of a wrecked car and shook her head. "This is awful. I hope no one died."

The front seat of the car was littered with shattered glass, and spots of—was it blood?—dotted the pavement. Jamie shivered, remembering what she had read about the Aztecs' religious rites. Blood, human blood—the tribal gods had demanded it. Maybe her mom had been right; maybe this case was too dangerous for them to mess with.

"We're wasting our time here, anyhow," she told Quinn. "This is just a traffic accident. What's this got to do with the mask?"

Quinn stared at her. "You saw the news clip. There was no reason for this to happen. And if the van with the skull-mask was passing by—"

"You think the mask just reached out and caused the truck to run into the other cars?" Jamie knew she'd raised her voice but she didn't care. "That's the dumbest idea I ever heard. How come you always think you know everything? Do you ever stop to listen to my ideas?"

"Jamie—"

She heard Quinn call her name, but she didn't stop to hear the rest of his remark. Anger was like a fog in her head, obscuring any other thought. This had been a waste of time, and she hated wasting time.

Turning, she stamped back toward the bus stop. But the stop was crowded with people, all staring toward the wreckage and the crowds gathering to watch the rescue efforts. Jamie continued to walk, her pace so rapid that she was almost running. She'd go back to the hotel and find a good book, or jump into the pool, or rent a video. When her mom came back, she'd tell Maggie that she wanted to go home, back to Los Angeles, and she didn't care if Quinn came with them or not—

Shocked at her own thoughts, Jamie stopped, and Quinn caught up with her.

"Jamie, what's the matter?"

She had come over three blocks in her rapid retreat, and Jamie realized she was out of breath. The anger slowly receded, and her mind cleared. She glanced at Quinn, glad that he couldn't read her thoughts. Or could he?

"I didn't mean it," she muttered.

"Mean what?" He looked at her, his expression puzzled.

Jamie sighed in relief. "I mean, I shouldn't have blown up at you like that. It just seemed as if we were wasting our time, and I thought—"

She stopped; she wasn't really sure what she had been thinking. At the time, it had seemed logical, but now she could hardly remember what had caused such intense anger.

"You must have gotten beyond its influence," Quinn said slowly.

"What are you talking about?"

"The skull-mask. It seems to affect people who are close by, causing arguments, violence even, in people who don't usually act that way. Remember what Manuel said—Antoine was his friend."

"You're saying I was affected by a stupid piece

of old gold?" Jamie shook her head. "Like it's cursed, or something? You're joking, right?"

Quinn met her eyes, his own gaze level, and Jamie looked away. "I was not affected by the mask," she repeated stubbornly. "I wasn't!"

"You got mad at me for no reason," Quinn reminded her. "And you wouldn't even discuss it. That's not like you."

Jamie bit her lip. "I didn't—"

"Come on, follow me, and try to stay calm. Don't let it take over your emotions," Quinn told her. "The van might have been caught in the traffic jam after the accident. Maybe it's still in the area."

He ran back toward the accident. Jamie hesitated. She didn't want to be left behind, but on the other hand, this whole idea was so dumb—

Unwillingly, she walked after him, then ran, trying to catch up. "You're on the wrong track," she muttered, feeling a wave of anger sweep through her again. "I don't—" Then she paused, shocked at her quick change of temper. Could Quinn be right? Was the skull-mask controlling her?

Taking a deep breath, she fought to clear her mind. She wouldn't allow herself to be used. "Where is it?" she demanded, no longer so sure that Quinn was mistaken. "Do you see the van?"

Quinn shook his head. "Let's try the side streets. It can't be far."

They turned away from the blocked main avenue and headed up the narrower street to the left. Even here some of the patrons of the small shops along the street had come out to peer curiously at the accident scene.

Quinn walked quickly around the people on the sidewalk, and Jamie kept up with him. She wanted to yell, "Slow down," then caught herself. This wasn't normal; she was usually more impatient than Quinn when they had a promising lead. Was this the effect of the mask, too?

Jamie shivered. It was as if someone else were trying to get inside her skin. She felt a wave of nausea and paused outside a florist to let her stomach settle. Maybe the sweet smell of the roses and the bright clumps of carnations would help her. She shut her eyes and took a deep breath, sniffing the fragrant aromas.

Then a sudden memory made her stiffen. Flowers—the Aztecs had loved flowers.

She opened her eyes and glanced quickly around. "Quinn!"

He had already gone ahead, but at her shout, he retreated swiftly. "What is it? Are you okay?"

"Let's check out the florist shop. The Aztecs had this thing about flowers." Why was he so dense, so slow to understand? She was babbling, trying to explain, fighting the wave of anger that again threatened to cloud her mind.

Without waiting to see if he followed, Jamie darted around the shop, through the narrow driveway and into the alley behind the florist.

She stopped abruptly. A brown van with a dent in its bumper stood in the back lot. Had it been hit in the multiple car crash? Perhaps the mask was too powerful for its own good.

Quinn gripped her arms. "Here, get out of sight."

He pulled her back, and they peered around the corner of the small building.

"Look," Quinn whispered. They watched as two men in the front of the van seemed to be arguing. One was small and dark-haired. Jamie remembered Antoine's description—was this the merchant sailor who had knifed his best friend over the golden mask? If so, who was the other man, the beefy man with the balding head, who seemed to be debating with Antoine?

As they both watched, the two men's voices rose until Jamie could hear scraps of their conversation through the van's open windows.

"Not enough money, you promised me—" Antoine was saying. "I will take it all myself, then—"

Scowling, he reached for the ignition key just as the bigger man reached into the back of the van and came up with a large steel wrench. Jamie gasped as he brought the wrench down, hitting Antoine on the back of his head. Antoine slumped over the steering wheel.

The big man opened the van's door and pushed Antoine's body out. Antoine fell limply to the pavement, and the other man slipped into the driver's seat. He revved the motor and turned the wheel. With a jerk, the van moved toward the rear of the alley.

"Look out, he's getting away," Jamie shouted. She ran forward, evading Quinn's hand.

"Wait," he yelled. "It's a dead end; didn't you see the sign? Don't get in the way, Jamie."

Too late, Jamie saw that he was right. The alley narrowed and ended with the back of another building. The van had no way to exit. The man behind the wheel saw the dead end, too. Brakes screeching, the van skidded to a stop. In a moment, the driver had turned the van; now he was coming back.

Straight toward Jamie.

8
Look Out!

Quinn saw the van turn, saw the frantic look on the driver's face. And he saw Jamie freeze, as if in shock, while the van sped toward her.

He ran.

The van was gaining speed. He'd never reach her in time. Everything seemed to be happening in slow motion, and he couldn't move fast enough.

"Jamie!" Quinn shouted, his voice shrill with desperation. Why didn't she move?

Only a few feet remained now between the van and Jamie's still figure. Her face was white, and her eyes stared blindly at the vehicle closing down upon her.

Quinn took a flying leap. He hit her hard, pushing her toward the side of the road. Propelled by the force of his blow, Jamie fell awkwardly to the pavement. But the impact seemed to awaken her from her trance. She scrambled up and ran toward the building.

Quinn tried to follow, but he couldn't get to his feet in time. The van loomed over him, and the driver wasn't going to stop. Quinn could see it in the man's set features, in the wildness of his eyes. Quinn couldn't breathe; he braced himself for the impact.

A man emerged from the doorway of the florist shop. It was Pajaro, and he held a gun. He fired at the speeding van—Quinn heard the sharp pop of the bullet—and the driver jerked the wheel.

The van swerved. Its wheels just missed Quinn, who rolled hastily away from its lethal rush.

The vehicle struck the side of the building, metal grating against brick, then it bounced off and continued down the alley. The driver turned so sharply into the street that the van lifted slightly, tilted on two wheels, then banged back down on all four tires and kept going.

Lieutenant Pajaro exclaimed sharply in Spanish, his chagrin obvious.

Quinn gasped. His hands and knees were scraped and bleeding, and his jeans were torn.

Lieutenant Pajaro paused to look down at him, still frowning. "Are you all right?" He tucked the gun back into a shoulder harness, out of sight once more.

Crouched on the pavement, Quinn nodded slowly. He could hardly believe he was still alive.

"You and your friend should stay out of this. It is too dangerous," the officer said. He glanced toward the street. "I must go now. There will be others coming, and I do not wish to be seen."

Quinn nodded in understanding, and Lieutenant Pajaro took rapid strides toward the main street, slipping away just as several people peered into the alley.

Quinn got to his feet, wincing in pain. Jamie came to help him up. Her face was still white and strained.

"Why didn't you try to move? I've never seen you freeze before," Quinn told her.

She bit her lip, her expression twisted. "I couldn't seem to think, Quinn. I was in a fog, lost, and the van didn't seem real. It was as if I were seeing through a veil . . . It was an awful feeling."

She shivered again. "Maybe the lieutenant is right," she said, very low. "Maybe we should stay out of this, Quinn. That mask is scary."

Quinn looked at her in surprise. Jamie had never wanted to give up a mystery before it was solved. She must be really frightened.

"If you say so," he said slowly. He thought of the mask leering at him in his dream. How could he be surprised at Jamie's fear? Anyone with any sense would be terrified of this thing.

"Quinn, Jamie! Are you two all right?"

At the sound of the shout, they both turned. Quinn recognized the voice right away. It was Nate Verdun.

Sure enough, the archaeologist had left his Land Rover at the entrance to the alley. He climbed out and hurried toward them. When he saw the blood on Quinn's hands, he frowned.

"We almost got run over," Jamie explained. "Quinn pushed me out of the way, and—"

Quinn threw her a warning look. The Mexican lieutenant didn't want his name mentioned.

"And he barely escaped," Jamie finished, understanding in her eyes as she nodded at Quinn.

"Are you hurt?" Nate bent over to look at Quinn more closely. His concern seemed genuine, and Quinn felt a flicker of guilt. He wanted to tell Nate everything—he didn't believe that the archaeologist had any ulterior motives—but Pajaro had saved Quinn's life. The least they could do was respect his wishes.

"I'm okay, just scrapes and bruises, I think," Quinn said.

"We'd better let a doctor check you out."

"We don't have time," Quinn argued. "The mask was here; we almost had it. Two men were fighting over it. One took off with the van and got away."

Quinn pointed to the limp body of Antoine, who still lay in the alley where the other man had pushed him out of the van. "I think that's Antoine," Quinn explained. "He had an argument with the other man, and he lost. But I know the skull-mask was in the van. I could feel its power."

So could Jamie, he thought, glancing at his friend. But he didn't say it. She was upset enough already.

Right now, he saw suspicion in her expression as she stared at the archaeologist. "How did you get here so quickly?" she asked.

"I was already on my way downtown when I checked my messages with my car phone," Nate said. "When I heard your message, I came straight on to Market Street. We'd better get the police to take Antoine, if this is him, into custody. Maybe after we question him, we'll find out who the other man is. Plus, they'll probably want you two to look at some mug shots."

Quinn glanced at Jamie, not sure she would want to be dragged further into the case.

But Jamie seemed to be recovering from her too-close encounter with the mask's strange power. "At the police station? Cool," she said with something like her usual spirit. "Let's go."

First, Nate checked Antoine, who still lay unmoving, then he walked back to the street and spoke to police officers there.

By this time, the more seriously injured victims of the multiple car crash had been transported to the hospital, and two policemen came back quickly to investigate this new incident.

They brought paramedics with them, and when one of the medical personnel checked Antoine, he shook his head.

"Concussion at the least, possibly a fractured skull," he said soberly. "We'll need x-rays." Motioning to his partner, they braced the unconscious man's neck and lifted him carefully into a stretcher.

"Take a look at Quinn. He was almost run down by a van," Nate told them.

While the second paramedic attached an IV to the unconscious merchant sailor, the first man looked at Quinn's scraped hands and legs, had him bend his neck and shone a bright light into his eyes. "No sign of any serious injury. If anything hurts later, come back and see us. You need to get those scrapes cleaned up."

Quinn nodded, wincing as the medic touched his sore hand.

"We'll stop at the hospital first," Nate suggested. "And we have to call Maggie and let her know what's happened."

Jamie swallowed, obviously thinking about what her mom would say.

Quinn shook his head. "I think we should go straight to the police station. All I need is a few plastic bandages and some soap and water," he said, determined to ignore the stinging abrasions. "And we can call Maggie on the way. She can meet us there if she wants."

And that way, maybe Maggie wouldn't forbid them to go the police station at all, he thought.

Jamie nodded. He could see that she wasn't in a hurry to face her mother's reproachful concern. "Yes, let's not waste any time."

They were soon in Nate's Land Rover and on their way. Nate located Maggie in the middle of a meeting at the studio. After a lengthy conversation, he seemed to convince her that Quinn and Jamie were all right.

"Yes, honestly, just a few scratches," Nate said into the phone, grinning at Quinn. "And I'll stick with them like glue, I promise."

When he hung up the phone, Nate looked across at Quinn. "She's upset, but she agreed that you should identify the man who tried to run you both down. The police are anxious to question you."

How much could he tell them, Quinn wondered. Lieutenant Pajaro didn't want to be mentioned, and Quinn didn't know whom he could safely discuss the foreign policeman with. And what about Jamie?

When they reached the police station, they were ushered through a busy room crowded with desks and computer terminals. They were led into a smaller office where two detectives listened closely to their story and questioned Jamie, then Quinn, about what they had seen.

"Can you tell me what this man looked like?" a short detective with friendly brown eyes asked Jamie.

She flushed, her face almost as red as her auburn hair. "I don't remember too much," she said, gulping. "I—I just couldn't think."

"Understandable," the policeman said, his tone soothing. A photo on his desk showed a smiling wife and three children, one probably about Jamie's age, Quinn thought. "You were in shock. It's okay."

But it was more than that. It had been the skull-mask at work, Quinn was sure of it. But he couldn't try to explain. The police were practical; they demanded hard evidence. They'd never understand the strange powers of the mask.

When Quinn's turn came, he tried to describe the man who had driven the van. "He was stocky, with broad shoulders and a round face. He wore a dark shirt, and he was balding. I couldn't really see his eyes. He was squinting."

"That's something." The policeman nodded in approval. "Good. Now we'll have you both look through our mug shots."

Quinn expected thick books of grim-faced men in black-and-white photos. Instead, they were seated before computers and allowed to examine one face after another.

Pretty soon, all the faces on the screen began to look alike. How would he ever know the right man when he saw him? Quinn was losing heart when he touched the button and another photo flashed across the screen.

"It's him!" Quinn exclaimed.

9
Clues

Detective Johnson came quickly to look over Quinn's shoulder. "Are you sure?"

"Yes," Quinn told him. "It's the same man who hit Antoine over the head and tried to run us down with the van."

The policeman punched another key on the computer and more information scrolled across the screen.

"His name is Tom Hefford, and he has a dozen different alias. He's a small-time fence with a lengthy criminal record, possession of stolen goods, small-time fraud, and the like. This is the first time he's been suspected of a violent crime." The detective shook his head. "We're going to have to assume he's armed and dangerous from here on out."

Quinn glanced at Jamie, who had left her own

computer screen to come and look over his shoulder. The archaeologist had been standing just behind, talking quietly with the detective. Now Nate came closer to look at the screen, too.

"Does that look like the man in the truck to you?" the policeman asked Jamie.

She narrowed her eyes, studying the computer photo. "Yes," she said slowly. "I think—yes, it is him."

"Good, we'll put out a bulletin right away," Detective Johnson told them. "Good job, kids. With Antoine still in a coma and not able to answer our questions, we really needed that identification. At least you've given us a chance to find this guy."

"And if we find him, maybe then we can recover the golden mask," Nate added.

Quinn wished he could forget Lieutenant Pajaro's lingering suspicions of the archaeologist. Of course Nate wanted to find the mask and return it to a Mexican museum, hadn't he said that all along? There was no reason to think Nate wanted the mask for any other reason.

Jamie shivered, and the policeman patted her shoulder.

"It's unlikely you'll see our Tommy boy again; he's likely long gone. I'd stay away from the docks if I were you, just to be on the safe side."

Jamie nodded, and Quinn wasn't inclined to argue.

Nate took them back to the hotel, and Jamie called her mom to tell her what had happened. When she hung up the phone, Jamie looked at Quinn.

He had flipped on the TV, but the flickering images couldn't hold his attention.

"Are you waiting for another news bulletin?" Jamie asked, sitting down on the other end of the couch.

Quinn frowned. Sometimes Jamie was too perceptive.

"You're right. I guess I expect something else to happen," Quinn told her. "The mask seems to cause violent actions wherever it goes."

"Do you really think it's affecting people? It's only a piece of metal," Jamie argued.

He looked at her, trying to read her expression. "But you should know, Jamie. You told me it was like being lost in a fog."

"But maybe the policeman was right, and it was shock—because I thought the van was going to run me down. Anyone can freeze, you know." Jamie sounded defensive.

And maybe she just didn't want to admit that she could have been affected by the mask's strange powers, Quinn thought.

"Look at Antoine, he'd never been in trouble before. Manuel said they were friends. Why did he turn on his friend?" Quinn asked.

"He was greedy; he wanted to steal the mask. He knew he could sell it for a lot of money," Jamie pointed out, sounding more like her usual practical self.

"And he ended up in a hospital bed, unconscious," Quinn reminded her.

"He didn't know that would happen," Jamie told him. "I still think—"

The sharp ring of the telephone interrupted her. Quinn reached to answer it. "Hello?"

"Is this Quinn McMann?"

For a moment he didn't recognize the feminine voice. Then memory rushed back, and he knew he had heard the slight accent before.

"Maria? Hi, how did you know where to find us?"

"When you took me home, Jamie told me where you were staying," Maria told him. "I—I'm afraid."

"Why? The same bullies?"

"No, no, we are having a neighborhood festival—usually it's a good time for everyone, food and family and friends, games and piñatas for the children to break. But this time—"

"What is it?" Quinn asked. "What's going on?"

"People are acting differently," Maria told him.

"Arguments without cause, old friends are not speaking to each other. We had two fistfights already. The party will go on all night, and I'm afraid what will happen. There's this feeling—this mood of anger—all for no reason."

"Maybe you should call the police," Quinn said slowly.

Jamie had come closer, trying to overhear the conversation. "What is it?" she asked.

Quinn whispered over the phone, "It's Maria. There's something wrong in her neighborhood."

Over the phone line, Maria's voice sounded strained. "And tell them what? That people are mad, that the party is falling apart? They would laugh at me. The police won't come until something bad happens, and then it will be too late. I don't understand what's happening, but I'm scared." Her voice shook a little.

Quinn felt the same cold touch of fear, and he knew why. "All right, we're coming. Give me the address."

He wrote down the street number she gave him, then hung up the phone. He repeated the rest of the conversation to Jamie, then looked at his map of San Diego.

"Do you think it's the skull-mask again?" Jamie asked. She frowned, her forehead creased with lines of worry. "But, Quinn, look—this is too close to the docks. You know what the police detective said. He told us to stay away."

"I wish I could," Quinn told her. "But we're the only ones who really know what we're dealing with. Like Maria said, the police won't understand. They won't believe that something bad will happen. But Maria was there before; she's already felt the touch of the skull-mask."

No one had felt it the same way Quinn had, but he didn't say that. He tried hard not to think it.

Jamie looked at him soberly. "This mask really scares me, Quinn."

"Stay here, then," he told her.

"Are you going?" Jamie bit her lip.

He nodded. "I have to. If I don't, I'm afraid of what will happen." And if the mask got stronger and stronger, Quinn thought, it would call to him from wherever it was, and he'd never be able to run away. Better to face it now.

"Then I'm coming, too." Jamie folded her arms. "I won't let you go alone."

Quinn pulled Nate's business card out of his pocket. He also had the slip of paper with Lieutenant Pajaro's number.

"Don't call Nate," Jamie said quickly. "He might tell Mom, and she'll have a fit."

"But we can't go by ourselves, Jamie," Quinn argued. "You just said how dangerous it is."

"Call Lieutenant Pajaro. He saved your life

once already," Jamie said sensibly. "Anyhow, he speaks Spanish, and Maria's neighborhood is mostly Latino. She told me when we took her home."

"All right." Quinn dialed the number and waited impatiently to hear a voice answer, but the phone rang and rang. Finally, an answering machine clicked in. Sighing, Quinn left a message. He hoped the lieutenant would check his machine soon because they had no time to waste.

"Come on, we'll have to get there on our own," Quinn told Jamie. He checked to make sure he still had the city map and money for the bus, then they ran for the elevator.

They waited for a bus at the corner. The city bus was crowded. Dodging an old lady's shopping bag, Quinn squeezed into the narrow aisle and held on to a metal pole. There were too many people around to discuss what they were going to do, and anyhow, Quinn didn't really have a plan.

Jamie stood a few feet away, frowning as she stared out the window at the busy streets. Was she as frightened as Quinn? Did she feel guilty, as he did, that they had gone out without leaving Maggie a note, and worse, gone somewhere she wouldn't have approved of?

But the skull-mask was just too dangerous to ignore. *What makes you think you can defeat it?* the voice inside Quinn's head said. Quinn tried to push back his self-doubt. He had to try. If he were as strong a psychic as his dad, he'd feel more confident, but Quinn was just learning to use his powers. If only his dad were still here . . .

Quinn shook his head, pushing aside the old sadness. He had to face the mask. Who else understood its power as he did? He had to try, whatever the outcome, or innocent people would be hurt.

Quinn looked at the map one more time, then stuffed it into his pocket. When he found the street he'd been watching for, he signaled to Jamie. They pushed their way through the crowded aisle and down the steps.

The bus pulled away with a puff of black smoke, and Quinn looked around him. He could already hear the loud, lively music of the block party, and banners hung from the nearest houses.

"This way," Quinn said. He and Jamie walked slowly toward the party.

"It looks like Olvera Street in Los Angeles during a Cinco de Mayo celebration," Jamie said. "Except not nearly as crowded."

Quinn nodded. He and Jamie and Maggie had visited the historical Los Angeles street earlier in the summer, and Jamie had explained the significance of the important Mexican-American holiday.

If he hadn't been warned, at first glance the scene all around would look festive and fun. People talked and held plates of food. At one side of the street a mariachi band dressed in wide sombreros and embroidered costumes played energetic music, and some couples were dancing. Nearby, two little girls ate ice cream, and several small boys tossed a ball back and forth.

Maybe Maria was worrying for nothing, Quinn told himself. Jamie tugged on his shirtsleeve, apparently with the same thought. "It looks okay."

"Let's walk around a little," Quinn suggested. They moved closer to the children just as one little girl dropped her ice cream cone. It rolled down her ruffled red dress, leaving a trail of chocolate. She wailed and stamped her feet. "You pushed me!" she said to her friend.

"Did not," her friend said. "You did it all by yourself, clumsy!"

They quarreled, pushing and shoving until a woman came to separate them. But at the same time Quinn saw a couple who had been dancing pull apart, arguing loudly in Spanish.

He shut his eyes and felt the undercurrent of anger, of repressed rage that floated among the party-goers like an invisible mist. The mask was here, he was sure of it.

Quinn shivered. He wanted to run far away from the skull-mask and its evil emanations. But it had to be found. As long as it remained in criminal

71

hands, it would continue influencing everyone in its vicinity.

"It's here," he told Jamie. "But not close by. We have to find it."

She nodded.

Quinn walked away from the shouting children and passed the band just as one of the guitar players hit the wrong note. A string broke, and he swore, and the other players stopped, too. As the music died, the people who had been dancing gathered around, shouting at the band.

"Hey, what's wrong, you have all thumbs?" a man in the crowd jeered.

One of the musicians turned around angrily, and a loud argument erupted, with people in the crowd taking sides.

"There's no reason for all this," Jamie whispered under cover of the noise around them. "These people are neighbors, friends. It must be the mask."

Where was Maria? Would they be able to find her amid the crowd? Quinn looked around. "Do you remember Maria's address?"

Jamie nodded. She pointed, and Quinn followed her lead. They slipped out of the milling crowd and headed toward the next street.

Jamie led the way to a small, neat stucco house with bright flowers in the yard. Before they could step up to the door, Maria ran out.

"You are here! I was at the party, but I had this bad feeling. And my mama, she has such a headache—she had to go home. She is lying down with a cloth on her head. What is happening at the fiesta?"

"Arguments, fights, just as you said," Quinn told her. "We have to locate the mask; it must be hidden somewhere nearby."

He shut his eyes, trying to feel the currents that swirled through his mind. When he opened his eyes, he found that he had turned west.

"This way," Quinn said. He walked rapidly away from the house, with Jamie and Maria following behind him.

When he turned the corner, he paused to close his eyes again and reach out with his hidden sense.

"Quinn, watch it!"

Someone pushed him roughly.

10
Back to the Docks

Quinn felt a sharp blow between his shoulder blades. He staggered and fought to regain his balance. Hitting a stucco wall at the side of the street, he felt the sting of the rough stucco on already raw hands.

Opening his eyes quickly, he saw the three teenagers from the dock. The leader was a big teen with longish dark hair. He wore a sleeveless T-shirt and baggy pants. His lips curled into a sneer.

"You are back again, Anglo, with no one to help you this time. Big mistake."

The other two laughed. Quinn felt a prickle of fear run down his spine. He didn't see any weapons, but there were three of them, all larger than Quinn. He braced his shoulders and faced them squarely.

"Look," he said. "There's no point to this."

"We don't like you," the first boy said. "Who needs a better reason, eh?"

"Leave us alone, Chico," Maria told him, her dark eyes angry. "We have things to do, important things."

"Oh, listen to the little girl," Chico said. He glanced contemptuously at Maria and Jamie.

Quinn took advantage of his momentary distraction to look around. The street was narrow, little more than an alley, with a tall wall on one side and a pile of lumber on the other, where someone was adding a room to a house. He saw no adults, no one who might come to their aid. It was up to him.

How could he hold off all three? Quinn felt his muscles tense, and his hands curled into fists. Maybe he could at least slow the teens down enough so that the girls could get away. From the corner of his eye, he saw Jamie back up just a little. Smart. Keep going, Jamie, he wanted to tell her. Make a break for it, take Maria with you. I'll delay them if I can.

He spoke so that Chico and his friends would focus on him and maybe not notice Jamie's retreat. "I don't want any trouble. We came for the party. Isn't that why everyone is out today?"

"No one invited you," Chico said, and the other

75

two nodded. "The party's a dud. But it's a good day for a fight."

Quinn saw the wildness in their eyes, and it reminded him of the van's driver, the man who had almost run him down. The skull-mask was still out there, still touching everyone close by with feelings of anger and aggression and hatred. Senseless violence, that's what the mask encouraged.

And these three seemed easy enough to sway. They had too much anger inside them already. Quinn could see it in their too-bright eyes, in the tight lines of their faces. And he felt it with his inner eye—that extra sense that he had always possessed. Anger moved like a red fog through their minds. . . .

Go, he thought, trying to send Jamie a message. Get away if you can, now. The feelings that emanated from Chico and his friends were growing steadily darker. The mask was doing its deadly work.

"We're going to make an example of you, smart boy," the tall teen said. He stepped forward, and his two pals stood just behind him.

Quinn raised his fists, pushing his own fear aside. If he ran, they'd be on him in an instant. He raised his chin and braced himself for the first blow.

Jamie had retreated out of his line of sight. But instead of running away, as he had hoped, she suddenly darted forward. Swinging a long thin plank, she hit Chico from behind, just at the level of his knees, and the tall teenager crumpled. The second boy was also hit, and he fell, staggering against the third. For an instant, they all lay in a confused heap in the street.

"Run," Jamie called, grabbing Maria's hand.

Quinn didn't hesitate to follow them. They took off down the narrow street. In a moment, Maria called, "There, through the yard."

She led the way across a scraggly lawn, then another, jumped a brightly hued flower bed, then ran up the next street. Quinn and Jamie followed as Maria twisted and turned through the neighborhood she knew well. They ended up on one of the wider, busier streets.

With no sign of the three teens, Quinn paused to catch his breath. The two girls stopped, too, panting.

"Pretty smart," he told Jamie. "Thanks, partner."

She grinned. "I have my moments."

Maria looked over her shoulder, her eyes still clouded with worry. "They will find us. Perhaps you should go."

Quinn shook his head. "Not until we find where the mask is hidden. It has to be near here."

They had circled the block party. He could hear the music again, and occasionally shouts. The feelings of anger and hostility were growing. Quinn couldn't walk away. Someone in the neighborhood might die if this senseless anger overflowed into violence.

"I have to go back," he told them. "You two should stay here."

Jamie shook her head, red hair brushing her shoulders. "I go where you go. You might need me."

He couldn't argue with that. Maria looked pale, but she came, too. They walked together back toward the mass of people, and Quinn tried to sense where the feelings of rage and hostility were strongest.

"Down there," he said suddenly, pointing to one of the alleys that crossed the main street.

Without waiting for the two girls, he turned into the alley and quickened his pace. He could feel the pull of the mask. It wanted him; it wanted his willing spirit.

Never! Quinn directed his thoughts toward the skull-mask. You're evil, whether made so from the beginning, or twisted somehow by human manipulation. You're evil, and I'll never accept your bondage.

He wanted to run the other way, but he had no choice. Quinn quickened his pace, and Jamie frowned as she struggled to keep up. Maria, who was the shortest of the three, was almost running.

After a time, the last of the small houses was behind them. Now Quinn saw a boarded-up store-front, then a small tavern, then the familiar fa-cade of large warehouses. They were back at the docks; how many blocks had they walked? He wasn't sure, only that the skull-mask was some-where nearby.

Maria looked around and shivered. "It doesn't feel good here, somehow," she said, almost whispering.

The mask was growing stronger. Did every act of violence, every blow or angry word add to its power? Quinn swallowed hard at the thought.

He stopped again and shut his eyes, reaching out to feel the currents that drew him toward the skull-mask.

A red fog drifted forward to engulf him. . . .

Quinn shivered and opened his eyes. "This way," he said. Walking quickly, he turned toward the docks.

He could smell the salty tang, the faint fishy odor of the water, oil, and diesel smells from the big boats and the trucks that passed along the street.

They could see large cargo ships and smaller

tuna boats in the distance. Quinn turned away from the commercial boats, and they all walked along the edge of the docks to a marina full of private vessels. Shining white yachts bobbed up and down in the water. Seagulls floated overhead, riding the air currents and screeching.

Quinn ignored the birds' shrill cries. A tall wire fence separated the marina from the public sidewalk, and the gate had a lock. But as they approached, he saw an older man, his hands full of grocery bags, unlock the gate and push awkwardly through.

Quinn ran up to catch the gate before it swung shut and automatically locked again. Already halfway down the walkway, the man didn't look back.

Quinn held the gate open and looked back at the girls. "You two go back and call Lieutenant Pajaro, and the San Diego police," he told them. He reached into his pocket for the Mexican officer's number and handed it to Jamie.

She passed the piece of paper on to Maria. "Can you get back without running into those bullies?"

"I think so," Maria said, glancing nervously over her shoulder. "I'll go to my aunt's house. Chico won't be looking for me there. And I can call the *policía*."

"Good." Jamie nodded at Quinn. "Let's go."

"But—this is dangerous, Jamie," he said slowly. "I don't think—"

"All the more reason you may need me," she argued. "Who saved your tender skin last time? Stop stalling, partner, let's move."

Quinn grinned ruefully and waved at Maria, who headed back the way they had come. It was true; he felt better when Jamie was at his side. They were partners, after all, the Mind Over Matter team. And he had no desire to face the golden skull-mask alone.

They walked together down the narrow pathway, past yachts and small boats of varying sizes. White decks sparkled, and well-polished brass fittings gleamed in the bright California sun. Everything was quiet and orderly and serene.

Jamie glanced at him. "Are you sure the mask is here?"

Quinn nodded. He could feel the lurking evil, the darkness behind the bright scene before them. Even the shifting water past the dock seemed darker than usual, and the gulls' cries more raucous.

He walked steadily, glancing at each boat, and he could sense the growing menace as they came closer and closer to the hidden treasure.

Why had the mask been hidden on a boat? He didn't know, but he was sure it was here, and every step took them closer to the most evil thing Quinn had ever encountered. He wanted to stop and run away, but someone had to face it, conquer the emanating evil that flowed from its cold metallic face. And those empty eyeholes—Quinn shivered at the memory.

He passed one more large white yacht, then stopped. The next vessel wasn't nearly as impressive as most of the boats tied up along the marina. Its decks showed patches of peeling paint, and the metal fittings were darkened with sea air and streaks of rust. The name on the side was faded.

"*The Pelican*," Jamie read aloud, her voice low. "This bird needs a good polish. Is it here?"

Quinn shut his eyes, then opened them quickly. The power of the skull-mask seemed to grow stronger every minute. How could he face it alone?

Maybe he should wait here for Lieutenant Pajaro, or for the San Diego police. Maybe it was stupid to go any closer. But the mask had powers that even the police would have trouble combatting. This time, Quinn might be the best prepared.

He had to go on.

"Hey, we're wasting time." Jamie's voice sounded shrill. Was she nervous, too?

"This is far enough. I want you to wait here,"

Quinn told her slowly. "When I go on that boat, I don't know what will happen."

Jamie frowned. Instead of answering, she backed up, then ran and jumped for the boat.

Quinn's eyes widened, but she made the deck easily, landing with a thump.

"What are you waiting for?" she asked, grinning, pushing her red hair back from her face.

Quinn frowned, but he, too, took a running jump and cleared the short expanse between the dock and the boat. He had to catch himself when he landed. The deck shifted slightly beneath his feet.

"Now what?" Jamie demanded.

Just like her to jump first and then ask questions, Quinn thought. "Now we find the mask," he whispered, "before anyone finds us."

Was there any crew on board? The upper deck seemed deserted. He didn't know much about boats. Where should they look?

Jamie glanced at the upper deck, then at him.

Quinn shut his eyes again to concentrate, though the mask's power seemed stronger every minute. He knew at once.

"This way," he said briefly.

They walked along the narrow deck until he saw the hatchway that led belowdecks. The opening looked dim, compared to the bright sunlight that splashed the outside of the yacht.

But the darkness inside was growing, Quinn could feel it. He didn't want to go down that narrow stairwell; he wanted to get as far away from this strange artifact with the haunting power as he could get.

But he had no choice.

"Down," he said.

11
Found

Jamie stood close to Quinn at the top of the narrow staircase. She saw him hesitate. Was it his old fear of closed-in places that made him reluctant to take the first step?

Or was it the mask itself that made him afraid to go deeper into the ship? Jamie didn't usually pick up psychic feelings; she was the matter-of-fact one, the scientific mind, and she was proud of that. But now even she could feel it—something not quite right—a brooding presence that made her want to look over her shoulder all the time, as if something threatening lurked in every shadow.

Quinn's expression was set, as if he fought the pull of the mask with all his energy. Maybe this was a mistake. Maybe they should go back. She was about to suggest a strategic retreat when Quinn visibly braced himself and plunged down the staircase. Anxious not to be left behind, Jamie hurried after him.

How strong was the skull-mask? What if it took control of Quinn? Jamie felt a moment of panic, then pushed the fear away. No, not Quinn; he wouldn't let that happen. What made her think such a thing? But she glanced at him nervously, new suspicions dancing at the edges of her mind.

When they reached the bottom, they were in a narrow hallway with closed doors along the side. Jamie felt the slight shift of the deck beneath her as the boat moved with the water, and somewhere she could hear a faint hum of machinery. Otherwise, the boat seemed very quiet. Where were the crew? Where was the man who had stolen the gold mask from its original thief?

Quinn looked back at her. "I don't hear anything," he whispered. "We'll try to find the mask and get out of here before anyone returns."

Nodding, Jamie tiptoed after him. They passed two doors, and she watched Quinn pause before each one, his ear pressed to the door to listen, just to be sure.

But all remained quiet. The sudden screech of a seagull outside the boat made Jamie jump, then sigh in relief when she realized what had made the noise. Inside, the hallway was still empty.

"Where's the mask?" she whispered.

Quinn motioned her onward. They went further down the passage, coming at last to a door at the very end. Quinn touched the doorknob. It turned under his hand.

When it opened, they saw another staircase, even steeper and narrower than the last, leading to the lowest level of the yacht. The whirl of machinery indicated that this was where they would find the engine that powered the vessel.

Quinn squared his shoulders and started down. Jamie followed right behind him. Halfway down her foot slipped on the narrow rungs and she caught herself on the guardrail. She gasped as she clung to the railing.

"Steady," Jamie murmured to herself. "Don't let this mask get to you. We can do this if we work together."

In a moment she found herself standing on a wet, oil-stained floor, a large motor chugging in front of them, and several boxes sitting along the side. One looked similar to the crates they had seen at the warehouse.

Quinn stood very still. He stared at the box, his expression hard to read.

"Is this it?" Jamie demanded, forgetting to whisper. Her voice squeaked with fear and excitement. Had they found the mask at last?

Quinn walked forward slowly. When he reached the crate, he hesitated.

Jamie found she was holding her breath. "Is it there?"

He touched the wooden lid as if it might burn him, then pulled hard. In a moment, it lifted. Quinn sat it down carefully on the damp floor of the hold, then reached inside the box.

All Jamie could see was crumbled paper. She came closer, afraid but fascinated at the same time. There—she saw Quinn touch a bigger mass, something firm wrapped in dirty burlap. Surely it had once been more carefully packed. Perhaps the thief had transferred it to this crate and wrapped it in this ragged cloth. Quinn lifted it— his face contorting when he touched it—and pulled the concealing cloth away.

Jamie gasped.

The golden mask was in the form of a stylized human skull, its empty eyes slanting slightly, and the mouth drawn up into a snarl. Just look- ing at it made Jamie shiver. So much fury was embodied in that taunting sneer, and the eyes— empty holes, really—but they seemed to look at Jamie, look deep inside where all the bad thoughts she had ever had lay buried. . . .

Jamie tried to look away, but the eyeholes held her, as if some spark of life were embodied in the mask itself—no, she refused to think like that.

She blinked, and when she opened her eyes again, she saw that Quinn's face was pale.

"Drop it," she said, hearing the hoarseness in her own voice. "Don't touch it, Quinn, it's evil."

"So many died," Quinn muttered, very low. He didn't seem to hear her. "The lines stretched up to the altar where the priests waited, with their knives ready, and the chief priest—his echo is still here—he enjoyed the killing, loved it, loved the blood—"

"Quinn, drop it!" She hit blindly at his arm, and he dropped the artifact back onto the box. He was shaking.

"Are you okay?" He looked as if he might pass out. She watched him take a deep, shuddering breath.

"There's so much death there. Some of them died willingly—they thought it was an honor, you know—but some were afraid. The priest—he didn't care about the gods he served, only about the power, and the blood . . ."

"Quinn, don't." Jamie felt her stomach roll. "How are we going to get that thing out of here? I don't think you should touch it again."

Quinn looked down at the grinning, snarling skull-mask.

The dull glint of the gold seemed very bright in the dim hold, yet it carried its own darkness with it, Jamie thought. Her knees still felt wobbly with fear.

Cautiously, as it were made of solid acid instead of gold, Quinn slipped the burlap bag around the mask, trying not to touch the artifact itself. When it was inside, he pulled the bag up and carried it gingerly by the edge of the fabric, with the heavy mask at the bottom.

"Come on," he told Jamie. "We'd better get out of here. The crew of the boat is bound to be back soon, and there's still Tom Hefford, the last thief."

She remembered the man who had almost run her down when he drove the van away—Jamie had no desire to meet that guy again. She nodded, and Quinn turned toward the staircase.

She followed just behind him, holding tightly to the rail. They were almost at the top when the door opened.

Jamie bit back a shriek of surprise. A big, burly man stood there, his balding head outlined against the brighter light. It was the man in the van. He held a large knife in one hand and he gestured toward them.

"You again! You bratty kids, why do you always get in my way? You think you can steal my prize?"

"You don't want it," Quinn said earnestly. "It's

evil. Look what happened to the first two men who had contact with it. It has a power—"

"You think you can scare me with mumbo jumbo?" Hefford laughed. "I'm not so stupid. This mask—it's going to make me rich. No more small-time jobs for me, crappy watches and VCRs and TVs—this is worth more than I could fence in a lifetime. And I'm not letting it get away. Get below, both of you."

He gestured with the knife, and Jamie backed awkwardly down the steps, managing not to slip this time. Quinn stepped down, too, very slowly, his gaze on the fence's contorted face.

What would Hefford do with them? Jamie stared at the knife in the man's hand and felt a cold knot of fear form in her stomach. He came another step closer. Then she realized that he was watching them, not the steps, and Tom was about to reach the rung where she had slipped earlier, the one with the oily patch.

She reached to clutch Quinn's arm, and he stiffened at her warning touch.

"Now!" She saw the man's foot slip, saw his heavy frame waver and topple, falling backward, then his heavy body bounced off the wall and he fell forward toward them.

She jumped to one side and Quinn to the other. Hefford hit the deck with a solid thud. For an instant, he lay still. The motor hummed noisily and almost drowned the man's groans. Then his body shifted. She didn't wait to see him get to his feet. Jamie ran, with Quinn just behind her. They hurried back up the stairs, clinging to the handrail so that they didn't fall on the slippery rung.

Hefford shouted, "I'll get you. You'll never get away with that mask—it's mine!" He must not have been badly hurt by his tumble because in a moment Jamie heard his heavy tread on the steps.

She and Quinn burst through into the corridor and ran toward the hatchway to the outer deck. The door was half open, and Jamie smelled the fresh, salty air beyond and saw the brighter glint of sunlight.

They were almost there, but Hefford's lumbering steps behind them sounded close, too close.

She heard Quinn gasp. Jamie turned and saw that the fence had grabbed Quinn's shoulder. The big man held Quinn tightly and tried to pull the sack from Quinn's hand.

"Get out, Jamie," Quinn shouted. "Get help!"

She didn't want to leave him, but when she looked around the narrow passage, she saw nothing to use against the big man. She would have to go on. If Maria had summoned help, maybe Jamie could lead the police back to save Quinn before it was too late.

She hesitated one more moment and saw Hefford tear the rough bag out of Quinn's grasp and push him to the deck. The big man turned toward Jamie.

Jamie ran. Despite the shifting deck, she was almost there. The opening was just in front of her, and she jumped through. For an instant, she had to catch her balance, then she looked around for the dock, ready to jump.

The space between the boat and the dock, which had been only a couple of feet when they clambered aboard, had widened—there was a gap of twenty feet or more. The ancient yacht was moving out to sea!

Now what? Jamie was a strong swimmer; she would have to take her chances in the water. She headed for the railing at the side of the deck, but a strong hand fastened around her upper arm.

Jamie swung around, her hand raised, but instead of the beefy Hefford, she saw the tall, thin form of Lieutenant Pajaro. He looked at her with concern.

"You? Where did you come from?" she exclaimed.

"I got the message, and I hurried here just before the boat started out. Where is Quinn? Did he find the mask?" the policeman asked urgently.

Jamie nodded, glancing over her shoulder. "He's behind me. But the man who stole it—the second thief—found us, and he has a knife."

Lieutenant Pajaro released her arm and reached inside his dark jacket. Jamie saw him pull out his gun and felt a surge of relief.

They both turned toward the passageway, and when Hefford appeared, holding the mask in its rough bag, she wasn't afraid. But where was Quinn? Had the big man hurt him?

No, he was right behind the fence, running to catch up, and his expression was grim.

"Jamie," he called, warning in his voice. "Look out."

"It's all right," she called, jubilant that help had arrived. "The lieutenant is here."

She nodded toward Lieutenant Pajaro. Then, to her horror, she saw him point the gun, not at Hefford, but straight at her heart.

12
Villains

Quinn drew a deep breath. Hefford laughed and pushed Quinn across to stand beside Jamie, who stared at the Mexican with an outraged expression on her face.

"But you're a policeman," she protested. "How can you do this?"

"I was *policía*, once," the tall man agreed. "They threw me off the force, for what do you say—corruption? But this—this will make my fortune for all time."

"And mine," the big fence said, a touch of unease in his tone. "I did the hard work, remember."

"Of course," Pajaro said smoothly. "First, take these two below. They must not interfere again."

He gestured with the gun, and Hefford gave Quinn a push, pushing him roughly backward.

Quinn caught himself with an effort. The boat was rocking more as it headed out across the harbor. Who was holding the wheel? How many men did Hefford have on board?

Jamie followed him down the steps, all the way back to the hold of the yacht. The oily smell and the pervading dampness seemed to have increased. Quinn could feel the wetness through his athletic shoes.

Hefford tied them both up with heavy twine, their hands behind their backs. The rope cut into Quinn's wrists when the man pulled it tight against his skin; Quinn tried not to wince. Once the bonds were secure, Hefford wrapped Quinn's rope around a metal post that braced one of the pipes. Jamie's wrists were tied, too, but he didn't bother to tie her to the post. He pushed her down next to Quinn.

"But you saved Quinn's life when the van almost ran over him." Jamie still stared at the Mexican as if she couldn't believe this sudden transformation. "Why?"

"So he would lead me to the mask, of course," Pajaro said. "I've been following the mask since it left Mexico. I have contacts who told me when the police discovered it here. And this boy—I knew he had powers, I sensed it. Then I saw him with the archaeologist. I followed you, later, until

I could arrange a meeting. You two were very helpful to me."

Jamie bit her lip and didn't answer.

Quinn felt anger and the cold touch of fear. No one would come now, until it was too late. Even if Maria had called the police, *The Pelican* was moving out into the harbor. The police would never reach them in time. Would the golden mask be their downfall after all? Was this the end of the Mind Over Matter partners? He felt a crushing sense of doom.

"Now," Hefford said, giving Jamie's ropes one more tug, "what about the money you promised me? Did you bring it like I said?"

"You think I carry two million dollars in my pocket, you fool? You will have it soon," Pajaro said. He reached for the burlap sack which the fence had laid carelessly on the damp deck.

The big man put out his hand and held on to the bag. "Not until I see the money," he said, his tone menacing.

"I must inspect the mask, first," Pajaro insisted. For a moment, the two men glared at each other. The atmosphere in the stuffy hold was charged with tension.

"I have to be sure it's the genuine artifact," Pajaro continued, his tone smooth.

"Okay," the fence muttered. He allowed Pajaro to open the bag and take out the golden skull-mask. Quinn braced himself, not ready to face the ancient idol's mind-bending powers again so soon.

The Mexican held it carefully, almost reverently. "Beautiful," he murmured, stroking the old gold, the snarling lips of the mask. "Such beauty, such power."

Watching him, Quinn shivered. As Pajaro touched the mask, the man's face altered and seemed to grow more savage. For an instant, Quinn saw—not a tall twentieth-century man wearing a dark business suit—but a fierce Aztec priest, gaudy in a brightly colored scarlet-and-blue-and-green feathered robe, grasping a sharp-edged obsidian knife. The man's eyes were tinged with madness, and his thin mouth twisted into a smile that made Quinn feel cold.

The mask was doing its deadly work, drawing out all the potential evil in Pajaro's heart, feeding on it, helping it grow darker and deeper.

The vision faded, but Pajaro still held the mask, stroked it softly, and crooned to it as if it were alive. Jamie was silent, her face pale, and even the big fence stirred uneasily.

"Hey, you put that back. You don't get the mask until I see my money."

For a moment, Pajaro didn't seem to hear, then he nodded slowly and lowered the mask to the deck.

"Of course. You will get what you deserve." He reached inside his jacket again and drew out—not money—but the small black gun he had pointed at Quinn and Jamie earlier.

"Hey, wait—" the other man said, his voice hoarse with fear, but it was too late. Pajaro fired, and the big man crumpled to the deck.

Jamie gasped.

Quinn found that he was holding his breath. Was the fence dead? No, not yet, Quinn could hear the rasp of his breathing, but the crook lay in a heap and didn't move.

Pajaro turned toward them, and Quinn tensed. But the tall man shook his head.

"No, too obvious, don't you think? We need to dispose of all of this—too much evidence." He put the gun back into the shoulder holster and walked across to the end of the hold, out of Quinn's range of vision.

What was he doing? Quinn heard a loud crash, like wood being split apart, then another, and another. When the noise ended, Pajaro came back and bent to pick up the mask. Before he slipped it back into the burlap bag, he paused to touch it. He caressed the age-worn surface, and again his face twisted.

Lost in his trancelike adoration of the ancient artifact, Pajaro didn't see Hefford stir, but Quinn did. He tensed as he watched the wounded man struggle to pull out his knife, but Quinn's hands were bound behind him. And anyhow, whose side could he take? Jamie watched, too, from beside him, but she didn't say a word.

Pajaro still didn't notice, not until Hefford's arm moved, and the knife flashed its silent path through the air. It hit Pajaro squarely and embedded itself in his chest.

Pajaro gasped and dropped the mask. "You— you—" He staggered, then fell backward, landing heavily on the steps.

Hefford moved, crawling toward the other man. Pajaro's eyes widened at this new threat. He tried to reach for his gun, but his right arm hung uselessly, and he couldn't easily reach his holster with his other hand. Hefford came closer.

Turning, Pajaro scrambled up the steep stairway, with the other man on all fours doggedly pursuing him. Hefford breathed with difficulty, and blood trickled down his shirt, but he followed Pajaro up the steps and out of Quinn's line of vision.

Quinn watched them go. The mask, almost forgotten, still lay on the deck. Water lapped its edges.

Water?

What had Pajaro done to the boat? The deck, always damp, now sloshed beneath several inches of water, and the engine snorted and choked in the background.

"Jamie," Quinn said, pulling at the thick rope that bound his wrists behind his back. "We've got to get out of here. I think the boat is sinking!"

13
Sinking!

Quinn pulled against the rope that bound him, tugged until his wrists ached from the strain and the friction of the rope against his skin. But the fiber was too strong, and the knots held. He couldn't do this alone.

"Jamie," he said, "if we can shift a little, I think you could reach the knots. If you can help me, I might be able to get loose."

"Why should I help you?" Jamie snapped, her voice tight with anger. "It's all your fault we're in this mess!"

Shocked, Quinn twisted to see her face. "What're you talking about?"

She glared at him. "If it weren't for your stupid psychic powers, we wouldn't be here, would we?"

"But—"

"I knew it was a mistake when you first came to live with us. I knew it wouldn't work. You've done nothing but cause trouble. First it was the mummy, remember? Then the haunted theater, now this—if it weren't for you, I wouldn't even be here."

"But you wanted to be involved," Quinn protested. It wasn't fair—how could she say these things? "I tried to send you back when I came on the yacht, but you insisted on coming along. You told me you liked solving mysteries. We're partners, remember? That was what you wanted."

"I was wrong, I don't want to be your partner," Jamie told him, her lips thin with anger. "And I don't want to be your friend."

The words hurt, all the way through, cutting just like the knife that Hefford had thrown at Pajaro. He'd never had a real friend before, not like Jamie. All his life, Quinn had been a loner, on the edges, laughed at or not trusted by the other kids. How could she turn on him like this? Anger suddenly flared inside him, replacing the hurt.

"You're a great one to talk, like you've never been in trouble before? What about that neighborhood bully who gave you such a hard time before I came? I helped you scare him off, didn't I? You didn't seem to mind having me around, then. And who are you—Miss Popularity? It's not like you've got so many other friends to choose from."

Jamie gritted her teeth. "You're a pig, you know that? Just because some kids make fun of my high IQ, at least I'm not a human freak—you know, the baby psychic. I bet you and your dad made quite a pair—"

"Don't you talk about my father!" Quinn shouted. "My dad helped a lot of people. Better than your mom, busy running around chasing any old news story—"

"You shut your mouth!" Jamie's face flushed almost as red as her auburn hair. "My mom is— is—the best reporter in the business, and if you—" She stamped her feet, and Quinn heard her sneakers splash wetly against the sodden deck. The water was still rising.

Water—Quinn glanced down. The ship was sinking. When he looked up again at Jamie, he blinked hard. For an instant, he saw the glint of gold reflected in her green eyes.

The mask!

The red-hot rage that had clouded his mind receded just a little. It was the mask, turning friend against friend one more time, just like on the cargo ship, when Antoine turned against Manuel and stabbed his old friend over the golden artifact. The mask drew out evil, just like the ancient priest who had imprinted it with his lust for power. It was the mask who had inspired this unthinking anger.

"Jamie, stop," Quinn said. He took a deep breath and tried to clear his thoughts. "It's not you talking. It's the skull-mask working on your mind."

As he said the words aloud, Quinn knew it was true, and his own anger faded. He looked at Jamie and really saw her this time, saw her clearly, not through a reddish fog of anger and hatred.

"You're my cousin, my friend, my partner," he said slowly. "I don't want to argue with you. Our friendship is very important to me, Jamie. And we have to work together. We can't waste any more time, or we're going to die, right here."

Jamie blinked at him, but he still saw anger in her face, and the blindness that rage brings.

"Fight it, Jamie," he urged her. "Fight the power of the mask. Remember our friendship, remember what we've been through together."

Slowly, her expression cleared. "Oh, Quinn," she said, her eyes wide as if she'd come out of a dark cloud. "I didn't mean what I said. I'm glad you're living with us now. I didn't mean it."

"I know," Quinn said, grinning in relief. "Now see if you can loosen these knots. We have to work together, now more than ever."

The water was past his ankles, and his jeans

clung wetly to his skin. Quinn twisted so that Jamie could reach his hands. He felt her tug at the knots.

But his bindings were still tight. What if this didn't work? Even if the police had been warned, they'd never get here in time. The water was up to his knees, now, and the engine sputtered.

"I don't know," Jamie muttered, her tone worried. "Maybe I can't—"

"There! I can feel it," Quinn interrupted. The bonds around his wrists suddenly loosened. He pulled hard, ignoring the pains that shot through his arms. "Yes!" He pulled one hand free, then another.

Turning, he reached for Jamie's wrists. The rope that bound her was wet now, and the knots harder to unloosen. But Quinn wouldn't give up. He eyed the water lapping at their legs.

Jamie's feet weren't bound, maybe they should get out of the hold now. But if the boat went down, she couldn't swim with her hands bound behind her back. Quinn pulled once more with all his strength, and this time the rope gave way.

"Yes!" Jamie pulled her hands free. "Oh, that hurts." She rubbed her arms as the blood surged back. "Let's get out of here."

Quinn nodded, and then looked back at the mask, now submerged in water. The gold glinted, and the eyeholes seemed to leer at him. He thought for an instant about how valuable it was, how old—how could they leave it behind?

"Quinn!"

Quinn shook his head. "Go," he said, turning his back with an effort on the golden icon.

They sloshed through the water and scrambled up the steps, then ran on through the corridor and up to the outside deck. Where were the other men?

As they plunged into the outer air, the deck shuddered beneath them. Quinn heard a boom that shook the whole boat. Something had exploded in the hold.

"Jump!" he yelled. Together, they ran for the side of the deck.

The water hit him, cold and salty, and he plunged deep beneath the surface. Behind him, red fire reached for the sky.

14
Partners

For an instant, the world seemed upside-down. Water was all around. Quinn shut his mouth tightly against the wetness. He couldn't breathe, and he fought against his old phobia.

Then he saw light above him, and the flickering flames of a ship afire. He thrust himself toward the surface.

When his face broke through the water, he drew a deep, shuddering breath, choking a little as he swallowed some of the bitter bay water.

"Jamie!" he shouted, treading water as he peered around him. The yacht was sinking rapidly, and now he saw a police boat heading their way from the side of the bay. "Jamie, where are you?"

At last, he saw a bedraggled mop of red hair

pop up only a few feet away. She swam toward him.

"Are you all right?" Quinn called, gasping.

"Yes." Jamie sputtered, too, trying to talk amid the choppy waves. "What happened?"

"Maybe the boiler exploded, I don't know. Look, there's a harbor boat. Over here!" Quinn yelled.

"Help!" Jamie added her voice to his.

The police boat was already putting out two smaller boats, and within a few minutes, strong arms pulled them aboard and wrapped blankets around them.

While the other skiff looked for more survivors—what had happened to Pajaro and Hefford?—the first boat took them back to the police vessel. When someone helped him up the ladder, Quinn's eyes widened.

Nate stood on the deck, side by side with the uniformed policemen. "Of course," Quinn told himself. If Pajaro's credentials had been fake, so had his warnings about the archaeologist. Still—

"How did you get here so fast?" Quinn asked. Nate led both the kids to the inner cabin, where someone poured them steaming mugs of hot chocolate.

"Maria had trouble convincing the police—it sounded like such a wild story. But when she mentioned the gold mask, and your name, the dispatcher called me. I got the harbor police onto it right away, and I came straight out. We were about to intercept the yacht when it blew up. I'm really glad to see you guys in one piece. Maggie would never have spoken to me again if you'd been hurt."

Quinn glanced at Jamie, who smiled reluctantly. Nate was an okay guy. Maybe after all this, Jamie would think so, too.

One of the officers called Nate away. He came back in a moment to share the news. "They've picked up three men from the yacht, two in pretty bad shape. But there's no sign of the gold mask. Do you know where it is?"

Quinn shook his head. "The last time we saw it, it was in the hold of the ship. It may not have survived the explosion."

Nate frowned. "That's a shame. It was an archaeological treasure. I'd hoped we could return it so it could be exhibited in a Mexican museum."

Quinn didn't answer. He shut his eyes for a moment, trying to sense an evil presence, but he felt nothing. Perhaps the mask had been blown to bits. Perhaps its lust for power, its ability to draw out anger and greed, would seep away beneath the cleansing ocean waters. Quinn hoped so. Nate didn't really understand how dangerous the gold skull-mask had been.

Opening his eyes again, Quinn glanced at Jamie. She nodded, as if following his thoughts. Jamie understood; she was his partner, after all, and his best friend.

"The police have a lot of questions for you," Nate said. "I'm going to give Maggie a call and tell her you're both okay."

When the archaeologist turned away, Quinn glanced at Jamie. "Want me to tell them what happened?" he asked her.

"Not without me," Jamie said quickly, finishing her mug of chocolate in one quick gulp. "We're a team, remember?"

Quinn grinned. "How could I forget?"

Even though they've successfully
warded off the skull-mask, our
intrepid investigators won't be able to
relax for long. Check out this preview of
Quinn's and Jamie's encounter with a
mysterious fortune-teller in

**MIND OVER MATTER #4:
THE GYPSY'S WARNING**

coming soon from Avon Camelot.

"I feel an unearthly presence!" Madame Celia waved her arms in the air. The layers of silver, enamel, and gilt bracelets around her skinny wrists clinked. The clatter was almost musical. The gypsy's voice, on the other hand, sounded deep and hollow. Her dark eyes were hooded by heavily-shadowed lids and her lips curved downward.

Jamie raised her brows and looked at Quinn. "What do you think?" she whispered.

Quinn lowered his voice, too, though the gypsy held everyone's attention, including the camera crew set up in the corner. The cameraman focused his lens on the dramatic figure in the long skirt and cotton blouse, whose hands flashed with big rings and whose strings of beads and golden chains tangled with her exotic-looking scarfs and shawls. She wore a turban on her curly brown hair; it was slightly crooked.

"I'm not sure," he murmured.

Jamie shrugged. "I think she's a fake. I don't know why Mom wanted to film her."

"You always say that. Anyhow, this will make a good segment for the show," Quinn reminded her. Recently, Jamie's mother had been assigned to a new evening feature news show, and she was always looking for unusual human interest stories.

Microphone in her hand, Maggie stood to one side of the gypsy. Her neat teal blue suit and small pearl earrings were a striking contrast to the colorful layers and flashy jewelry that the gypsy wore.

Behind them, the director spoke quietly and the cameraman turned to focus on Maggie. She spoke into the mike. "Maggie Anderson reporting, taking a look at a psychic exercise. This is Madame Celia." She nodded toward the gypsy. "She's rid three houses of ghostly beings, or so she says. Of course, the Pacific Heights area of San Francisco is filled with old houses with colorful pasts.

"Now that Marian Van Cliff, widow of the noted financier Norman Van Cliff, has bought this nineteenth century mansion in order to restore it to its former glory, she too has detected an unwanted spirit in residence. Mrs. Van Cliff has brought in Madame Celia to banish the ghost from the house."

Maggie paused, and the cameraman shifted back to the gypsy while the soundman moved the portable boom so that the news report would pick up Madame Celia's voice. She was chanting in a language that Quinn didn't recognize. First she lowered her voice, mumbling foreign words beneath her breath. Then suddenly she shrieked dramatically, throwing her hands up.

Jamie jumped. "Do you feel anything?" she whispered to Quinn. "Any ghosts or spirits hanging over us?"

Quinn shook his head. "Something isn't quite right, but—I don't feel a ghost."

He didn't sense anything in the room. And he should be aware of a ghostly presence, detecting it with that extra sense that was so hard to explain to other people. He'd had that ability for years, just like his dad. Roark McMann had been a famous psychic; before his death he had aided police and insurance companies in solving tough cases. That was what Quinn wanted to do, too, when he grew up. Or maybe before.

He looked around the room again. The gypsy was still chanting, her eyes half-closed as she sat on an old Victorian chair—the chair had good vibes, she'd said. Mrs. Van Cliff sat nearby on a more comfortable modern chair, watching the gypsy's performance anxiously. Next to the widow, her sister, Katrina, perched on the very edge of her chair, looking nervous and unhappy.

Mrs. Van Cliff's nephew by marriage, Rodney Van Cliff, leaned against the bookcase behind her. He was short, with long hair and modish clothes, and his expression was scornful. Another man sat to the side, an older man with graying hair and dark-framed glasses; he was Tom Horne, Katrina's friend. His expression was hard to read; he had a shaggy graying mustache that helped mask his expression.

Madame Celia raised her hoarse voice again. "I have made contact," she said. "It was difficult, but I have located the secret spirit. He is standing beside the right-hand window!"

IF YOU DARE TO BE SCARED... READ SPINETINGLERS!

by M.T. COFFIN